"I Promise I Won't Expect You to Marry Me,"

Susan said. "Not even if my reputation's completely ruined."

Smiling slightly, Adam leaned down to kiss her cheek before releasing her hands. Then he took a step backward, but his eyes never left her face.

"It doesn't seem very fair, does it?" he asked solemnly. "It seems to me that if we're going to be gossiped about anyway, we may as well really be enjoying a torrid affair."

Though his seemingly serious tone made Susan's breath catch in her throat, she managed to whisper, "Is that a proposition?"

"Maybe," he whispered back. "If it were, would you accept it?"

DONNA VITEK

firmly believes that "I would probably have never learned to enjoy writing as much as I do" without the helpful influence of her husband, Richard. This is her third Silhouette Romance.

Dear Reader:

Silhouette Romances is an exciting new publishing venture. We will be presenting the very finest writers of contemporary romantic fiction as well as outstanding new talent in this field. It is our hope that our stories, our heroes and our heroines will give you, the reader, all you want from romantic fiction.

Also, *you* play an important part in our future plans for Silhouette Romances. We welcome any suggestions or comments on our books and I invite you to write to us at the address below.

So, enjoy this book and all the wonderful romances from Silhouette. They're for *you!*

Karen Solem
Editor-in-Chief
Silhouette Books
P.O. Box 769
New York, N.Y. 10019

DONNA VITEK
Promises from the Past

Silhouette Romance

Published by Silhouette Books New York

America's Publisher of Contemporary Romance

To my husband, Richard

Other Silhouette Romances by Donna Vitek

A Different Dream
Showers of Sunlight

SILHOUETTE BOOKS, a Simon & Schuster Division of
GULF & WESTERN CORPORATION
1230 Avenue of the Americas, New York, N.Y. 10020

ISBN: 0-671-57066-8

First Silhouette printing March, 1981

10 9 8 7 6 5 4 3 2 1

Promises
from the Past

Chapter One

"You can't stay here, Miss," the guard said in a loud whisper, smiling apologetically. "I'm sorry, but they don't allow visitors in the studio while they're taping. If they let one in, pretty soon more come and nobody can move around, there's such a crowd. I'm going to have to ask you to leave."

Susan Thomas smiled at him as she tucked a strand of shoulder-length dark hair behind her ear. "Will you let me stay if I tell you my cousin asked me to wait for her here? You see, she's in the commercial they're about to tape, and she thought it would be all right for me to stay and watch."

After looking her over carefully, the guard finally returned her smile and nodded, obviously satisfied that she was not simply someone who had wandered in from the street. "Okay, if your cousin said it would be all right, then I guess it doesn't matter, as long as you're very quiet and don't bother anybody."

"Oh, I won't, I promise," Susan assured him as he walked away.

To make certain she was out of the way, she moved closer against the partition that formed a three-sided room in the vast expanse of the studio. Far back behind the cameras and the bustling crew, she looked around curiously. She had never watched a commercial being filmed before, and she was grateful to Barbara for bringing her along this afternoon. Though she realized her older cousin's invitation was undoubtedly an attempt to ease her own conscience, she still appreciated the gesture. Besides, she thought Barbara was wrong to feel guilty anyway; nobody was really responsible for what had happened. There was no way Barbara could even have imagined that the position she had found for Susan on an Atlanta newspaper would fall victim to the publisher's budget trimming at the last minute.

Perhaps it had all been too good to be true anyway. One Thursday Susan had been busy scouting out the local news for the Forest Falls, Georgia, *Gazette,* and on Friday she had been frantically packing her bags to catch a bus to Atlanta.

That had been over two weeks ago, and the glow that had shone in her lovely violet eyes as the big-city adventure had begun was beginning to fade now. Actually it had begun to fade that first Monday morning when she had gone to see Barbara's friend at the newspaper and been told that the position she wanted no longer existed. Even then she had not really been unduly upset, thinking she could find a similar position on another of Atlanta's newspapers. Unfortunately, she had soon learned she was only one of many reporters looking for work, and she became just another name on the long lists of applicants. Discouraged but not defeated, she decided to find something else temporarily, but landing an interesting job that also paid enough for her to get her own apartment was proving much more difficult than she had imagined. Now, after two weeks of countless disappointing and usually impersonal interviews, she was beginning to yearn for Forest Falls and the sense of belonging that comes with seeing familiar faces every day and knowing exactly where she fit in the scheme of things.

This morning had been particularly discouraging. The first interview was a complete waste of time when she learned neither the pay nor the work environment was anywhere nearly as terrific as the employment agent had led her to believe. She was not at all interested in taking the position when the personnel manager finally admitted the salary was low and the duties far from stimulating. But the second interview had been a different matter altogether. A position on the staff of a regional magazine with a large circulation sounded almost as good as reporting for a newspaper. Unfortunately, the managing editor did not feel as enthusiastic about her. After a quick glance at her résumé, he had said rather icily and pompously that she was far too young and inexperienced to become one of his staff and the agency had wasted both his time and hers even sending her to see him. As a result of his unfriendly attitude, she had left his office feeling more than a little inadequate and rather country-bump-kinish, since he had nearly sneered at her small-town newspaper experience.

Now, as she watched the members of the production crew scurry around the set, that feeling of inadequacy increased considerably. It seemed everybody had work to do except her. Hoping to make herself as inconspicu-ous as possible, she moved closer to the partition, taking care not to trip over the thick electric cables that crisscrossed the floor. Thrusting the memory of the debilitating morning to the back of her mind, she watched as several men pulled a huge white raised disk before the lights and cameras, then removed the dollies beneath it.

After only a few more minutes and a great flurry of activity, Barbara and several other people appeared. At least, Susan was reasonably sure she recognized her cousin. But it was difficult to tell, since all except one of the people now on the white circular platform were costumed head to ankle in narrow lengths of dark beige foam rubber. Only their faces peeked out through oval openings. They were supposed to be French fries, accompanied by the one exception, a man whose arms, legs, and head extended from an amazingly realistic-looking foam-rubber hamburger with lettuce and tomato peeking out around its edges.

It was undoubtedly the strangest sight Susan had ever seen, and she grinned broadly at the thought of sophisticated, *soignée* Barbara wriggling her tall slender form into a foam-rubber French fry.

As she watched, a harried voice suddenly boomed out a command for quiet and the bustling activity around the set ceased immediately. Six takes later, patience seemed to be wearing thin all the way around, and Susan, who had not had lunch, was wondering how much longer it was going to take to finish. Shifting her weight to one foot, she switched Barbara's portfolio from one hand to the other. Then, as she listened to the director make his latest complaints, a sudden uneasiness stole over her, a certain sense of being watched closely. Looking around, she stared straight into the eyes of a tall, slim man standing on the other side of the set. For a moment she was able to meet his intense, speculative gaze directly; but when the corners of his mouth lifted slightly in a smile, she returned it, then looked away.

Even then, however, the uneasy sensation did not subside. For several long, uncomfortable seconds she could still feel his eyes on her. Finally she looked around again, but this time both the man and his woman companion were staring at her as they talked quietly.

How very rude, Susan thought disgustedly, her cheeks warming with embarrassment. What could they be finding so fascinating about her? Forcing herself to resist the urge to check to see if her slip could be showing, she gazed straight ahead. But now she felt far too self-conscious to pay real attention to the taping.

Ignoring the temptation to simply leave the studio, she stayed where she was, becoming increasingly uncomfortable with each passing second, until, out of the corner of her eye, she saw someone approaching. It was the woman who had been staring at her, and Susan forced a polite but puzzled smile as she came to stand beside her. Without returning the smile, the woman lifted her hand lazily, indicating in a gesture that she would speak to Susan during the next break in the taping.

Something haughty in the lifting of her arched eyebrows irritated Susan immensely. If there was anything that really antagonized her, it was snobby, supercilious people—and simply the set of this woman's mauve-tinted lips screamed snob. From the top of her stylishly coiffed short blond hair to the tip of her snakeskin shoes she looked every inch a lifeless manne-quin. As Susan watched her run an unnecessary smoothing hand over her plum-colored suede suit, she sighed inwardly, wishing she knew what the woman could possibly want with her.

At last they were between takes again and the woman turned toward Susan, her eyes sweeping over her simple indigo wrap dress with what seemed to be disdain.

"You're not supposed to be in here," she announced unceremoniously. "This is a closed set. You should be waiting out in the hall."

"But my cous—"

"And you won't do at all anyway, you know," the woman interrupted. "Your agency obviously misunder-stood the requirements, because you're nothing like what we asked for. You're much too short, not at all sophisticated, and we did ask specifically for a blonde."

Completely confused now, Susan shook her head. "I'm afraid you've made some kind of mistake. I don't—"

"No, honey, you're the one who's made the mis-take," the woman interrupted rudely again, and impa-tiently this time. "Or your agency did."

"But I—"

"Why don't you just run along? You're not at all what we had in mind, so there's no need wasting your time waiting around here. Of course, if you'd like to leave a photograph from your portfolio with your name and address, we'll file it and if we ever need someone of your type—"

"Oh, but I—"

"Please do as I ask." Waving her hand in a grand, sweeping gesture, the woman thinned her lips out in an attempted smile. "As you can see, we're extremely busy here."

"Yes, I know, but—"

"Just leave your photograph on the receptionist's desk across the hall," she commanded as she turned to walk away.

After watching her go out the studio doors, Susan glanced around, as if seeking someone who might listen to her explanation, but obviously no one had witnessed the confusing scene. Even the man who had accompanied the woman was no longer in sight.

Her Majesty might have at least let her get a few words in, she thought grumpily. Then she shrugged, determined not to allow one impolite woman to make her feel any worse than she already did. But after the beating her ego had taken this morning from that tactless magazine editor, she had really not needed to be told she was too short and completely lacking in sophistication.

"Those two should be married," she muttered softly to herself. "They deserve each other."

"May I have a word with you?" a deep voice behind her suddenly asked. "We seem to have something of a mix-up here."

Susan spun around but, unluckily, as she tried to take a step backward her heel caught on one of the electric cables. Had it not been for the pair of strong hands that shot out to grip her upper arms, she probably would have sat down clumsily on the floor. Murmuring her thanks, she looked up into the face of the man who had been staring at her only a few minutes ago. From a distance he had not seemed quite this tall, and she had not really been able to see that his seemingly blond hair was in reality almost silvery, though he could not have been older than his mid-thirties.

With an embarrassed smile, she pulled free of his grasp. "You startled me a bit," she said softly. "I had no idea you were behind me."

"Obviously," was his amused answer, as his emerald-green eyes inspected her from head to toe, then met her own directly. "I apologize for creeping up on you, but I felt I should come and straighten out this mistake personally."

"Mistake?"

An apologetic smile gentled his tanned, rugged features as he gestured toward the studio doors. "My colleague, Miss Brooks, has just spoken to you, I believe, about the apparent misunderstanding we had with your agency."

"Well, yes, she did speak to me, but I had absolutely no idea what she was talking about."

"I thought you must have been a little confused." His smile deepened as he took a step closer, lowering his voice to a whisper as another take of the commercial began. "Nellie doesn't always take the time to explain matters as clearly as she could, I'm afraid, so I thought I'd better come and give it a try myself. I know it's terribly inconvenient for you, coming downtown for nothing, and I apologize. The agency—"

"But you don't—"

"Have you just recently arrived in Atlanta?"

"Well, yes, but—"

"I thought so. That's it, then. I expect someone at your agency probably filed your photographs under the name of another one of their new girls, undoubtedly a tall blonde. That may be exactly why you were sent here by mistake."

Sighing, Susan shook her head. "I don't belong with any agency. You see, I—"

"Ah, you just heard we were looking for a girl for a new campaign and decided to drop by and see if we'd be interested in you," he murmured, taking her elbow. "I understand now."

"No, you don't!" she whispered urgently, holding up Barbara's portfolio for him to see as he gently but relentlessly steered her toward the doors. "I can't go. I have to stay here and—"

"But you'd just be wasting your time," he whispered back. "Let me explain. This series of ads calls for a worldly young woman. And our client insists she be a blonde." A flicker of impatience tightened his jaw momentarily when she opened her mouth to protest again. "Look," he continued, "why don't you just leave us a photo and your name? Then, if anything else ever comes up that—"

"But I'm not interested in anything else!" she interrupted finally in desperation. "I just want a chance to—"

"And you wouldn't believe how many other girls want that chance too," he persisted, his hand tightening around her arm, turning her to face him when they reached the doors. "Can I give you some advice? I know you came to Atlanta expecting to find success immediately, but it rarely happens that way. It takes time, so you'll have to learn to be more patient, especially since tall, willowy blondes are all the rage these days. Many of our clients request that we use blondes in their ads. And you aren't really that tall, either. Besides, you look very young. How old are you anyway?"

Jerking her arm free, Susan glared up at him, but, to her dismay, the feeling of inadequacy she had experienced since the disastrous morning interview suddenly overwhelmed her. Tears filled her eyes so quickly that she could not lower her lids fast enough to conceal them. With a muffled exclamation of frustration, she turned to jerk open one of the doors but was stopped in her escape by gentle hands descending firmly on her shoulders.

"Wait a minute; don't run off all upset," he whispered comfortingly. "I didn't mean to sound so discouraging."

Now was the time to explain the crazy mix-up, but Susan was far too upset to care if this infuriating man ever learned her real reason for being in the studio.

"Just let me go," she demanded, her teeth clenched tightly together. "I'll take myself and everything that's wrong with how I look right out of your sight."

"But there's nothing wrong with how you look. I just said you're not especially tall and very young—"

"Never mind; I heard you the first time," Susan snapped at him, her eyes flashing. "Now let me tell you something if I can without your interrupting. I have no desire to work for you. I wouldn't be involved in one of your stupid ad campaigns for all the money in the world, not if it meant I had to deal with you and that ridiculous snob of a woman who was in here a while ago. Besides, who in his right mind would ever want to be cast as a French fry!"

Her outburst obviously irritated him immensely, considering the anger that suddenly lit his green eyes. His strong fingers dug into the muscles of her shoulders. "If you feel that way, then I don't think you need leave your name and photograph on your way out after all," he said stiffly. "If I were you, I'd just go home and cool off."

"I'd be glad to, if you'd be so kind as to let me go," she retorted, twisting free, then swinging around so quickly that the corner of Barbara's portfolio struck the man's knee.

Cursing beneath his breath, he grabbed her by the

wrist before she could get through the doorway. "I'd advise you to learn how to control your temper, little girl," he whispered furiously. "Your attitude isn't going to get you anywhere, I assure you."

"And I'd advise you to take your hands off me right this minute, you big jerk!" Susan responded, in a much louder voice than she had intended. And even as she regretted responding so violently, an ominous silence fell over the entire studio. She looked around, groaning inwardly as she realized that everyone in the vast room was watching with avid interest her exchange with this man.

"My, you certainly know how to make a good first impression, don't you, honey?" the man remarked cruelly, a little smile curving his lips. "I don't think now would be the best time to introduce yourself to the director and ask him if he'd be interested in working with you sometime."

Susan met his mocking smile directly, mustering the little bit of dignity she still possessed.

"Then, if you'll be good enough to release my hand, I'll get out of everybody's way," she said tersely, despising herself for the slightly quavering quality in her voice. And when the man's fingers pressed suddenly against the delicate bones of her small wrist, the look in her wide, bewildered eyes became more beseeching. "Please," she whispered. "Just let me go, please."

He released her immediately, then started to speak, but she rushed out the doors before he had a chance to utter another word. It was difficult to restrain herself from running down the hall, but she managed to do it somehow. She had never been so relieved to see anything in her life as she was to see the opening elevator doors when she turned down the corridor to the right.

Mercifully, she was the elevator's only occupant and, as delayed reaction made her legs tremble weakly, she clung to the handrail as she was carried up to the building's top floor before the descent began. Then she waited, breathless with dread, as the numbers on the panel lighted individually down toward the six, the floor she had just left. "Oh, heaven, don't let it stop," she whispered pleadingly. Only when the light behind the five flashed on did she take a deep, tremulous breath.

In a hurry to escape, she was out on the street and halfway down the block before she realized she still carried Barbara's portfolio. Stopping dead in the middle of the sidewalk, she provoked an uncomplimentary comment from a man who nearly stumbled over her from behind. But she hardly noticed.

Now what was she going to do, she wondered in a panic. She could not go back up to that studio, that much she knew; but Barbara would kill her if she ran off with the portfolio. After taping the commercial, Barbara had a very important appointment with an executive of a large advertising agency that seemed to be very interested in her. So she would have to have the photographs in the portfolio before that interview.

Turning back reluctantly, Susan trudged along, trying to think what she could do. As she went back into the lobby of the building, she saw the solution to her problem.

Running cautiously across the slippery marble floor, she caught up with the guard she had talked to in the studio just as he pressed the button for the elevator.

"Excuse me, but do you remember me?" she asked, laying her hand hesitantly on his arm. "I'm afraid I've done the silliest thing. I had to leave before the taping was finished upstairs and I completely forgot to leave this portfolio for my cousin. Now I can't take it back up to her, and I wondered if you'd be kind enough to take it for me."

Surprisingly, the guard shook his head. "Guess I better not do that, miss. Miss Brooks just told me a minute ago to see you didn't get back in here again. So

I don't think she'd want me running errands for you, neither."

Susan's cheeks were burning as she looked down at the floor. This seemed to be her day to be humiliated, and she longed to go lock herself into Barbara's apartment. But before she could do that, she had to get this portfolio up where it belonged.

"Please," she muttered, looking up again. "This really wouldn't be a favor for me—my cousin has to have these photos for an interview she has this afternoon. Wouldn't you be willing to take them up, just for her sake? Surely Miss Brooks wouldn't mind your running an errand for her."

"Well, I don't know," he said, stroking his chin indecisively as he looked her over speculatively. "You know, I was really surprised to hear how much of a ruckus you caused up there in the studio. You sure didn't seem to me like the kind of little girl who would want to do that."

Susan shrugged. "I'm not sure how it all happened myself—it was mostly a stupid misunderstanding that just got out of hand. But, really, I'm not usually a troublemaker; it's just that it's been a horrible day."

"Some of them are, that's a fact," he said agreeably. Then he grinned. "Oh, all right, honey, I'll take them pictures up to your cousin for you if it's that important. But I don't reckon you better show yourself around here any time soon."

"I understand," Susan said, handing him the portfolio before he had a chance to change his mind. "My cousin's name is Barbara Thomas, and she's tall and pretty, with blond hair."

"Ain't they all?" he answered wryly. "But I'll find her, don't you worry. Now, just get on out the door before Miss Brooks comes down here and catches me talking to you. That woman can have a real mean mouth sometimes."

Murmuring her thanks, Susan hurried away, not

wanting to chance causing trouble for him with the overbearing Nellie Brooks. She wouldn't wish that woman on her worst enemy, much less on the only person who had treated her kindly all day.

At least Barbara's problem had been solved, but as Susan walked out again into the early autumn sunshine she felt terribly tired and depressed. Now she could see how childish her reaction to the man in the studio had been, and she wished she had taken her frustration out on Nellie Brooks if she had had to take it out on anybody. Actually the man had attempted to be nice, but, upstairs, she had thought his attitude was extremely condescending. It had not helped matters in the slightest that he, like the obnoxious Miss Brooks, had never given her a chance to explain what she was really doing in the studio.

Yet why should she care, she asked herself as she crossed Peachtree Street to wander aimlessly into the park. She had no ambition to be a model anyway. But his faultfinding had wounded her despite that fact. No girl wanted to hear an attractive man tell her she was not sophisticated or tall enough—or, in other words, not pretty enough. She had to be honest with herself— the man in the studio had been attractive. And she had not wanted him to say he did not think she was.

With a tremulous sigh she sank down on a bench that faced a small fountain and adjusted the sides of the center slit of her sand-colored skirt so that less thigh was exposed. Maybe she simply did not belong in Atlanta, she considered pensively as she stared blindly at the clusters of red berries that clung to the branches of the dogwood trees across the path. The people here did seem much more indifferent. In Forest Falls, everybody had been interested in everybody else and it had been nice to know they all cared. Maybe she belonged with people like that, people who were not so afraid to show their concern for one another.

Yet she had only been in Atlanta for two weeks, she

reminded herself as she got up to walk on. Surely she would not allow the few unfriendly people she had encountered today to sour her on the entire city. Most Atlantans probably were not so blasé and indifferent.

Besides, she was no quitter—she never had been. She would forget what had happened today and start fresh again tomorrow. Her spirits revived, Susan's steps became bouncier as she hurried along, and she refused to even think about the events of the morning. But she stopped short suddenly when she heard a noise coming from the thicket of trees that bordered the path. Tilting her head to one side, she listened, and in a moment she heard it again. It sounded like a soft moan, and this time it was followed by a loud fit of coughing, then labored breathing. Lifting up a small branch laden with reddening maple leaves, she peered into the shadowy copse and saw an elderly man clinging weakly to the trunk of a tall pine tree.

As she went to him, the leaves that had already fallen to the ground rustled and crunched beneath her feet so that he heard her approach. Holding out his hand, he whispered a raspy thank you as she took it. But he didn't seem too steady on his feet, and she released his hand to slide her arm around his waist.

"Put your arm across my shoulders," she told him. "Lean on me and I'll get you to a bench."

"No, I'm too heavy," he said, wheezing.

"Really, it'll be all right," she assured him. But when he draped his arm over her shoulders to lean heavily on her, she realized that his gaunt appearance was misleading. He weighed more than she had imagined.

But she was determined not to let him fall and managed to stumble out of the trees with him, urging him along to a bench about twenty feet away. He sank down gratefully onto it.

As he closed his eyes and rested his head against the back of the bench, she looked him over. He had to be in his seventies at least, and his clothes hung loosely on his thin body. Concerned about the lack of color in his cheeks and his quick, erratic breathing, she bent down to touch her fingers against his hand.

"Do you think you'll be all right? I'm going to find a phone and call an ambulance."

His fingers suddenly caught her own in an amazingly tight grasp. "No, I don't need an ambulance, don't want one," he whispered, opening his eyes slightly. "Just sit with me a minute while I catch my breath. I guess I tried to walk too far."

Since his fingers still held on tightly to hers, Susan had no choice except to do as he requested. But she managed to free her hand to loosen his tie and unfasten the top button on his shirt. That seemed to help. Within a few minutes, he was taking deeper breaths with less frequency and the color was slowly coming back into his cheeks.

"Dratted old age," he muttered crossly. "It gives me a pain." Then a mischievous twinkle lit his blue eyes. "Gives me several pains, in fact."

When he cackled merrily at his own joke, Susan smiled too. He was obviously feeling much better and that was a great relief to her.

"Surely getting older must have its good sides too," she offered logically. "It can't be all bad."

"Maybe not; I guess there are some benefits," he conceded. "But at moments like this, I can't seem to remember what any of them are."

"Would you like me to see you home? I'd be glad to. Or, if it's too far to walk, I can get you a taxi."

"I'm not ready to go home yet. Just sat down." He grinned at her. "Besides, a man my age doesn't get many chances to sit in the park with a pretty girl like you. But you look mighty young. Why aren't you in school?"

"Heavens, I don't look that young, do I? I finished high school long ago. I'm twenty-one years old."

"My goodness, that's ancient," he teased. "And

what's your name?" After she told him, he eyed her speculatively. "Any relation to the Michael Thomas who lives out near Covington?"

"No, I don't have any relatives near Atlanta. My cousin Barbara lives here, but she's only been here about two years."

"Just got here yourself?"

"Two weeks ago."

"You liking it?"

Susan shrugged. After the morning she had endured, to say she was wild about Atlanta would be an outright lie.

"Some things I like, some I don't," she answered evasively. "It's hard to get used to everything after living in a small town all your life. How about you? Do you like living here?"

"Actually I don't live right here in town. My place is about ten miles out, but I did work for nearly fifty years right over there." He pointed in the direction of the building Susan had just left. "And, you know, I still can't get used to doing nothing after coming in to work every day for so many years." Shaking his head rather sadly, he took off his glasses to clean the lenses with a crisp white handkerchief. "Where do you work, honey? Someplace nearby?"

"I'm afraid I haven't found a job here yet," she told him, trying not to sound too discouraged. "My cousin thought she had one lined up for me, but it fell through at the last minute so I have to look for another one." Then, as he questioned her further, she found herself telling him about almost every interview she had had in the past two weeks. In fact, she told him everything that had happened to her, excluding the dreadful scene in the studio, of course. The fact that she had allowed herself to be goaded into such a foolish fit of temper was not something she was eager to broadcast.

When she had finished, he sat silent for a long moment, tapping his forefinger against a lined cheek.

"Tell you what," he said at last. "I know some folks in the newspaper business. Why don't I talk to some of them about you?"

Susan smiled at him, grateful that he wanted to help, but she did not really imagine he knew anybody with enough influence to do her much good. "It's very nice of you to want to help, but I wouldn't want to put you to any trouble."

"No trouble at all. I'll give Bob and Henry both a call when I get home." Pushing himself up, he got to his feet, then stood looking around curiously. "Speaking of home, I guess Baker's beginning to wonder where I am. I better go find him or I'll never hear the end of it. But before I go, you write down your address and phone number for me, in case I have some luck with Bob or Henry."

After he insisted, Susan gave him Barbara's address and number, though she felt writing it down was a wasted effort. However, it was such a little thing to do to make him feel as if he might be able to help her find a job.

An unusually cool breeze for late September was blowing as Susan walked with him toward the west exit of the park. She noticed that he shivered slightly and stuffed his hands into his trouser pockets after brushing back the shock of white hair from his forehead.

What a nice old gentleman, worrying about her finding employment when he probably had to survive on a small fixed income and could not afford to buy anything warmer than the rather worn sweater he now had on. Yet that was the way it was sometimes. Those people with the least wanted to give the most while those with the most, like the obnoxious Nellie, would not even try to be civil to strangers.

Pondering the injustice of it all, Susan almost walked past the exit.

"This way, honey." The old gentleman prompted her with a gesture that she should precede him through the wrought-iron gates. She stopped on the sidewalk, meaning to ask him how he would get the ten miles home, but just as she opened her mouth to speak someone behind her shouted.

"Lord have mercy, Mr. Joshua, you had me worried sick!" another older man chided as he trotted up to them. "Where you been? I been looking all over that park for you."

"Hush your fussing, Baker, and meet Miss Susan Thomas. She came to my aid when I had a little weak spell."

"Weak spell?" Baker exclaimed, his fat hand reaching out. "Hold on to me now, Mr. Joshua. I'll get you right to the car."

"Hah! That would be a little like the blind leading the blind, wouldn't it, Susan?" he asked with a laugh that ceased almost immediately when Baker grumbled indignantly. "Oh, all right, you can help me to the car if it'll make you feel better." Grimacing endearingly, he looked at Susan. "Baker here thinks he's my mammy."

"He needs one too, Miss," Baker retorted. "And I want to thank you for seeing him back to the car. One of these days, though, mark my words, he's going to wander off and have a spell and nobody's going to know where he is. But you can't tell him a thing. No, sir. Mr. Joshua Thornton knows more than his doctor, more than me, more than anybody else in the—"

"Oh, that's enough," Joshua Thornton interrupted. "Let me say good-bye to this young lady; then you can fuss all you want on the way home. Not that I'll listen to a word of it," he whispered to Susan as he faced her again. "Now, could Baker and I see you home?"

"Oh, no, I can catch a bus right on the corner. Thank you anyway."

"Well, I want you to know how much I appreciate your coming to my rescue. And I promise I won't forget to call Bob and Henry about you as soon as I get home."

"Thank you," she murmured, smiling slightly to herself. "You take care of yourself from now on, all right? Let Baker know where you're going."

When Joshua nodded and Baker walked over to open the door of a gleaming black Mercedes parked at the curb, her smile faded abruptly. Joshua Thornton waved to her after settling himself in the front seat, but she simply stared at him for a moment before having the presence of mind to return the wave.

Then they were driving away and she was gazing rather sillily after them. Who could have guessed that the rather sad-looking old gentleman was obviously much more affluent than he appeared? And as Susan wandered off toward the bus stop she began to wonder exactly how influential Joshua's friends Bob and Henry might actually be. But she supposed it really did not matter. He might forget to keep his promise to call them anyway.

Chapter Two

That evening, Susan had already had her bath and was curled up lazily in an easy chair reading when Barbara came home about six o'clock. When she heard the key in the lock, Susan laid her book aside to get up and pad into the kitchen to check the stew she had put on earlier to simmer. Sniffing the appetizing aroma appreciatively, she started to take the plates out of the cabinet to set the table but nearly let them slip out of her hands when the front door slammed shut with a loud bang. Then, when a muffled curse followed a suspicious thud, she thrust the plates aside and ran back into the living room.

"Oh, heavens, Barbara, I thought you had fallen," she said breathlessly. "What was that awful thud I heard?"

"My tote bag hitting the floor, I imagine," her cousin answered stiffly, striding across the room to stare out the window.

"I hope there wasn't anything in it that would break," Susan said as she walked over to pick up the bag. "Don't you think you better check inside? If your makeup bottle broke, any clothes you have inside will be ruined."

"I guess I'd better, then, hadn't I?" Barbara snapped, turning with a flounce of her skirt. "All I need is for that white silk blouse to be covered with makeup."

When her cousin came to her then and snatched the bag from her hands, Susan's eyes mirrored her surprise. And, as she watched her drag the contents piece by piece from the bag, then toss them carelessly on the sofa, she frowned bewilderedly.

"I bet you're hungry, aren't you?" she finally asked with forced cheerfulness. "I've made that stew you used to like so much for Mother to prepare when you came to visit us. She taught me how to make it so that it tastes just like hers. You won't be able to tell the difference."

"I won't be having dinner here tonight," Barbara muttered as she examined the bottle containing her makeup. "I'm going out."

"Oh, you have a date. Is it with that intern you've been hoping would ask you out?"

"No. I'm just going to a movie with some of the girls I work with."

"Oh. Oh, I see," Susan murmured. But she did not see at all. It was not like Barbara to go out with her girlfriends without asking her to go along. But, obviously, tonight she was upset with her and it was not very difficult to imagine why. Taking a deep breath, Susan gestured helplessly. "You're mad at me, aren't you?" she asked unnecessarily.

"Why, no! Why on earth should I be mad at you?" Barbara responded sarcastically. "After all, you didn't do anything but embarrass me in front of my friends, plus ruin the ninth take of that idiotic commercial. Do you know it took eight more takes before we finally got that darn thing right?"

"I don't think you can blame all that on me, though, can you?" Susan offered softly. "After all, I just messed up that one take. It was the director who didn't like the sixteen others."

"Well, maybe so," Barbara conceded reluctantly.

"But you certainly can't tell me you did absolutely nothing wrong!"

"I didn't say that."

"And I should hope you won't try to!" With an exasperated cry, Barbara slapped back a straying strand of her thick blonde hair. "Oh, boy, if I could have gotten my hands on you before you left that studio, I think I could have wrung your neck. What in heaven's name came over you? I've never seen you act that way. What made you pick today to have your first temper tantrum?"

"I was provoked."

"But why did you have to take it out on *him?* Of all people in the world, why did you have to pick him to call a 'big jerk'? And why did you have to say it loud enough for all Atlanta to hear it?"

Suppressing a smile at the look of horror on her cousin's face, Susan gestured apologetically. "I didn't mean to say it so loudly, but I did mean to say it. That man is a jerk."

Barbara laughed dramatically. "Oh, you think so? You think *he* is a jerk? Would you like me to tell you exactly who he is?"

"I don't much care who or what he's supposed to be. To me, he's still a jerk."

"Well, that jerk is Adam Kincaid, probably the top account executive for Mills, Simpson, and Thornton, the biggest advertising agency in Atlanta. And they happen to have offices everywhere. If I could do some work for them and they liked it, why, I might find myself in New York in no time flat."

"What's that got to do with what I called him?"

"I'm just trying to make you understand who you were insulting, Susan! I'm sure Mr. Kincaid knows all the big wheels in this town. If he happens to tell any of them how you acted, your chances of getting a job are zero."

"But, Barbara, he doesn't even know my name. How could he hurt me?"

"You're sure he doesn't?"

"I don't see how he could. I certainly didn't say, 'Hi, I'm Susan Thomas, and I think you're a big jerk.'"

"Oh, how can you be so flippant? What if someone tells him that I'm your cousin? Oh, I'd just die."

"Thank you very much," Susan muttered, her eyes darkening unhappily. "I'm sorry you're so ashamed of me."

"Now, I didn't mean it that way," Barbara said hastily. "It's just that I'd hate to lose a chance to do some work for Mills because you had an unpleasant encounter with Adam Kincaid."

"And I'd hate for that to happen too. But I don't think it will. I bet Kincaid forgot all about me before I could get out of the building."

"I wouldn't be so sure of that if I were you. Judging by the grumpy, rotten mood he was in when I talked to him this afternoon, something was making him angry—and I have a feeling it might have been your calling him a big jerk right in front of all those people."

Susan shook her head confusedly. "But why were you talking to him this afternoon anyway? From what you just said, I got the impression that you didn't know him."

"I don't. I mean, I didn't." Barbara sighed impatiently. "Don't you remember me telling you I had a very important interview this afternoon?"

"Yes, of course I do. That's why I sent your portfolio up by that guard."

"Well, you silly, that interview was with Mr. Kincaid! I've been trying to get one with him since I came to Atlanta. And what happens the day I finally get it? My own cousin makes him so mad that I know he was hardly listening to anything I said to him. And he didn't even bother to look through my portfolio. He just told me to pick out the photo that I thought made me look the most sophisticated and leave it with him."

"Sophisticated?"

"Of course. He's looking for a girl to do a series of ads for one of Mills's clients, a world-famous jeweler. Mills is screening girls in New York, Houston, and San Francisco. If I could just get lucky and they picked me, I'd have it made, Susan."

Everything was falling into place now.

"And this client insists on a tall, sophisticated blonde?"

"Yes, but how did you know?"

"So that's what he thought I wanted," Susan said musingly. "I had no idea what he was talking about."

"And I have no idea what you're talking about!"

Leaning forward, Susan propped her elbows on her knees and cupped her chin in her hand. "It started with that snippety Nellie Brooks. There I was, not bothering a soul, watching you tape your commercial, and here she comes, telling me I have to leave because I'm too short and not at all sophisticated. She didn't even give me a chance to tell her I wasn't there for the reasons she obviously thought, but I knew she'd just made a mistake so of course I didn't leave. Then here he comes, taking my arm and acting as if he's going to drag me out. And all the time he's telling me I'm too short and unsophisticated. Well, I'm telling you, Barbara, that magazine editor this morning had made me feel low enough. I didn't need people telling me what was wrong with how I looked, especially when I didn't ask a thing from them to begin with. He wouldn't even give me a chance to explain that I was just there to watch you." Susan shrugged. "One thing led to another, and before I knew it I was calling him a big jerk. But I really didn't mean for anybody else to hear that."

"Why couldn't you have just stayed calm? He didn't mean anything personal by what he said. Models get talked to that way all the time. If you're not what the client wants, they tell you why, like your hands are too big or your mouth's not just right."

"Well, I'm not a model," Susan said heatedly. "And I expect people to be polite to me. If they don't like the way I look, then I'd appreciate it if they'd keep it to themselves since I can't change the fact that I'm short and have dark hair and an obviously unsophisticated face."

"But he didn't mean anything personal," Barbara persisted but to no avail.

"I don't care what he meant. It was terribly rude to drag me toward the door that way without giving me a chance to explain who I was. Every time I opened my mouth, he interrupted me. And that woman, that Nellie, she was worse; she didn't even make an attempt to be nice at first."

"Oh, she's that way with all the girls. Nobody can stand her. For the life of me, I can't understand how she's such a successful space buyer for Mills with that rotten personality of hers. But maybe she doesn't act that way when she deals with the salesmen and the magazines and newspapers."

"Well, I could have done very well without having her intrude in my life today. She couldn't have picked a worse time."

"No, she certainly couldn't," Barbara muttered petulantly. "I just wish you hadn't lost your temper. It would have been nice to talk to Mr. Kincaid when he was in a better mood."

"I'm sorry if I had anything to do with making him so grumpy," Susan said earnestly and calmly, even though she no longer felt calm. The tranquil mood she had finally managed to attain this afternoon after she came home was gone again. Now she felt as out of place and ignorant as she had all morning. And there seemed to be only one way to avoid these feelings. "You know, I think maybe I should just go back home," she added quietly. "I'm beginning to believe I must be one of those people who really don't belong in a big city."

"But you've only been here two weeks!" Barbara protested vehemently. "You can't go home yet; you haven't given yourself a chance to get accustomed to the way things are here."

"Oh, Barbara, I can't even find a job. I'm just a name near the bottom of the list of applicants at all the newspapers. No, it seems pretty silly to stay here if I can't even find a job I like. Besides, this apartment's very small—pretty soon you're going to get tired of stumbling over me all the time."

"You let me worry about that," Barbara said emphatically. "You know I don't mind having you here or I wouldn't have invited you in the first place."

"But when you invited me, you had no idea I'd go around calling influential men big jerks, did you?" Susan asked with a wry little smile. "And maybe you're right. It probably wouldn't help your career any if that Kincaid man knew you are related to me."

"Oh, I really didn't mean that when I said I'd die if he found out you're my cousin!" Barbara cried, her expression anguished. "It was such an ugly thing to say and I'm so sorry. Let Adam Kincaid find out you're related to me. I don't care if he does."

"But I do. Why should you have to suffer because I reacted like a silly little girl?"

"But it was very rude of him to drag you toward the door that way."

"Maybe so, but he can afford to be rude, can't he? Unfortunately, I can't. And I think you'd have to classify calling someone a big jerk in front of a crowd of people as extremely rude."

"Well, I guess the best thing to do is just try to forget the whole thing ever happened. And that's just what we're going to do tonight." Barbara stood, a no-

nonsense gleam in her eyes. "I'm going in there and switch off that stew of yours. Then you're going to throw some clothes on and go with the girls and me to a movie."

"But I don't—"

"I don't want to hear any excuses. Get up from there and go get dressed."

But Susan stayed where she was. "Could we go out tomorrow night instead?" she suggested hopefully. "I know you're trying to cheer me up and I really appreciate it; but, really, I don't feel up to a movie tonight. What I'd like to do is sit here quietly and think of some places I could go to look for a job the rest of this week, because I think that's what I'm going to do—look for one more week, then go home if I haven't found something I like."

"But I hate to leave you alone when you've had such a rotten day. I'll just call Becky and tell her I'm not going to the movie."

"No, you won't. I'm a big girl and I can stand to be by myself. You made plans and I don't want you to change them because of me."

"Are you sure?" Barbara persisted. "You won't be lonely?"

"I'm sure."

Yet, a half hour later, after Barbara had left, the apartment did seem rather empty. For a few minutes Susan wandered through the rooms aimlessly; then finally, with an impatient sigh, she sat down cross-legged on the floor and opened the evening newspaper to the want ads. Out of this long list of available jobs, surely there had to be a few she would enjoy doing, but she had already discovered in the past two weeks that many of them sounded much better in the ads than they did when she actually talked to someone about them.

"Ah, well, maybe I'll get lucky," she said aloud as she put a circle around another great career opportunity. Then the phone rang, and she stretched back to lower it to the floor beside her before lifting the receiver.

It was the old gentleman from the park, Joshua Thornton, which surprised Susan. She was certain he had forgotten all about her as soon as they parted.

"I've just sent Baker into town to pick you up," he said immediately. "I want you to join me for dinner, so you better start getting ready right now."

"But, Mr. Thornton, I don't think I'd better come tonight," she protested politely. "I'm nowhere near ready to go anyplace."

"It shouldn't take a beautiful girl like you long to make yourself presentable."

"I see you're not above using flattery to get what you want."

"That was not flattery, young lady, and you know it. Now, say you'll come, please. I live in a fine old antebellum house that old Sherman overlooked and I know you'd enjoy seeing it."

It was the word *please* that defeated her resolve to stay home. Though he had tried to keep his tone light, the loneliness she had detected in that one word had been painfully obvious.

"All right, you win, Mr. Thornton; I'd be happy to come."

"Wonderful," he enthused, laughing happily. "And after dinner I want to talk to you about a job possibility."

"Oh, really? You mean you've already talked to one of your friends?"

"I'll explain everything when you get here, which you'll never do if you don't go get ready. See you in a few minutes."

When he hung up Susan sat for a long moment, the receiver in her hand, staring in amazement at the floor. Life certainly was strange sometimes. But when she realized she had no time to ponder its mysteries now, she leaped up and ran into the tiny bedroom, where she rifled through the closet. Deciding she should dress up for the occasion but not too much, she chose one of her favorite dresses, a midnight-blue jersey that darkened her violet eyes to an even more exotic hue and highlighted the sheen of her dark hair, which she wound into a loose chignon on her nape.

After smoothing a tiny amount of blusher onto her smooth ivory cheeks, and touching up the mascara on her lashes, she surveyed herself in the mirror. The low V-neckline of the dress looked a bit too plain, so she clasped on her favorite piece of jewelry, her grand-mother's ornate gold locket.

All in all, she had to admit she did not look bad, considering the few minutes it had taken her to get ready. But as she examined her reflection critically, she suddenly wrinkled her nose and sighed. Rude as Nellie Brooks and Adam Kincaid had been this morn-ing, they had both been absolutely right. There was not one iota of sophistication in her small oval face. Maybe it was those wide eyes. Turning her head slightly, she half closed her lids and cut her eyes toward the mirror. But she discovered that the ploy only made her look a little silly, rather than seductive and provocative as she had hoped. Giving up the attempt, she turned away from the mirror in disgust and wandered into the living room. And, only a moment later, as she looked idly through a magazine, there was a knock on the door.

"Ah, there you are, miss," Baker said, wiping a handkerchief across his brow. "I had a devil of a time finding you. All these apartment buildings look alike to me." Folding his handkerchief again, he tucked it into his pocket as he stepped into the living room while Susan picked up her purse. "There's a cool wind tonight, miss. I expect you better wear some kind of wrap."

After she went for her black tailored jacket, he

helped her put it on. "We better be off now, miss, before Mr. Joshua gets impatient and decides to call over here to see if we've left yet."

As they pulled away from the curb a few minutes later, Susan gazed out the window from the back seat of the Mercedes, wondering what Barbara would say if she could see her right now, being chauffeured away in such grand style. Settling back, she enjoyed the smooth ride as Baker took the interstate toward Neenan, but after only three or four miles he turned off the highway onto a tree-lined secondary road that twisted and climbed into the Appalachian foothills. They passed only a few cars and, with the scrub pine and browning blackberry thickets edging the road, there was an illusion of isolation that made it difficult to remember that a busy metropolis was only minutes away.

Susan felt the tensions of the day slipping away as they drove on into the dark silence. By the time Baker turned the car into a white-pebbled drive, she was humming softly to herself and strumming her fingers against the seat, eager to reach their destination.

She did not have much longer to wait. Over a gentle rise in the drive and around a sharp bend, the house sat in a semicircle of maple and pine trees, and magnolias and dogwoods were scattered liberally over the front lawn. Some of their leaves were gone now so that their branches were beginning to look bare, but the cold, stark picture they presented only made the sprawling house seem warmer in comparison.

The house was not the typical restored plantation mansion. It was white with a columned veranda that was not quite centered, as if additions had been made to one side of the house and not the other. That gave it more character, Susan thought, and she could hardly wait to see inside.

A middle-aged woman in gray uniform with white ffs and collar ushered Susan in, but before she could even help her off with her jacket Joshua Thornton came into the wide entrance hall and waved her away with a mischievous grin.

"Do you know how long it's been, Emily, since I helped a young lady out of her coat? It seems to me that you'd let me have that honor this time since it's not every day I have a beautiful guest for dinner."

Emily returned his grin as she slipped Susan's jacket back up over her shoulders. "There you are Mr. Joshua. Play host if you want to."

With an exaggerated flourish, Mr. Thornton bowed stiffly from the waist before Susan. "Welcome to Maiden's Bower, Miss Thomas. I can't tell you how honored I am to have the pleasure of your company this evening."

Smiling, Susan curtsied. "And I can't tell you how honored I am that you invited me, Mr. Thornton."

"I must say you look absolutely ravishing tonight."

"Even though you only gave me ten minutes to get ready?"

His eyes sparkled merrily. "I told you a beautiful young lady could make herself presentable on very little notice. And that's the true test of beauty, you know. Anybody can look attractive if they spend all day working at it."

"I still say you're an outrageous flatterer," Susan retorted over her shoulder as he helped her with her jacket. "What would you have said if I had arrived here with rollers in my hair?"

"But you didn't, and I never feared you would. Now, would you care for a drink before dinner, or shall we just go on into the dining room?"

"I don't care for a drink, thank you, but I'd be happy to join you if you would like to have one."

After looking all around, he leaned closer. "I'm afraid I have to do all my drinking on the sly these days," he whispered. "My doctor has forbidden it, and that wretched Emily watches me like a hawk."

"Then I guess we'd better just go on in to dinner," Susan whispered back.

It was a delightful meal, though she paid very little attention to the delicious food Emily Baker served them. She was much too busy listening to the fascinating stories Joshua Thornton told her about his family. They had lived in Maiden's Bower since the early 1840s, and it sounded as if every one of them had known full, exciting lives, most of them respectable. One of the exceptions, however, had been the original owner, Jonathan Thornton. At thirty-five he had been wounded in a duel by his nearest neighbor, who sought to avenge Thornton's ruination of his daughter, Felicity. Defying her father, Felicity had nursed Jonathan and subsequently married him; but even after forty years of being the perfect wife and loving mother, she had died with a still-soiled reputation.

"It must be terrific to know so much about your family, to know what they were like and how their lives turned out," Susan commented as they settled themselves in the sitting room after dinner. "It's so exciting knowing that some of the things in this very room actually belonged to Jonathan and Felicity."

"You're really interested in things like this, aren't you?" Mr. Thornton asked very seriously, squinting his eyes as he watched her face. "You're not bored when I talk about my family."

"Of course not! How could anyone be bored hearing about Felicity and Jonathan? What a romantic story."

"I'm glad to hear you say that, because I have a proposition to make you. Just wait," Mr. Thornton said excitedly, getting up to hurry across the room to a large oak secretary, where he took out a carved wooden box. Then he came back to sit down beside Susan, balancing the box on his knees. "Now, first I want to tell you I didn't forget my promise this afternoon. I did call both my friends, Bob and Henry, about the possibilities of getting you a job on one of their newspapers, but I'm afraid I didn't have much luck. Both of them said they're operating on very tight budgets and simply cannot take on any new reporters right now."

"Yes, that's what I heard everywhere I went."

"*But* Bob told me he would definitely keep you in mind if anyone on his staff quits any time soon."

Nodding, Susan smiled resignedly. "I appreciate his doing that, but I really need a job right away."

"I know you do, and that's why I'm about to make you this proposition," Joshua said, digging into his pocket and bringing out a small key to unlock the box he held. Inside was what looked to be a ledger bound in soft brown leather. "This was my grandfather's journal. For years I've been thinking about using it as a guideline to write the history of my family, but I never seemed to get around to it. Now, when I have all the time in the world to work on a project like that, I find I just don't have the energy to deal with all the details that would be involved. But if I had someone to help me . . ."

"And you were thinking I might be able to?" Susan asked incredulously. "Oh, but I've never done anything like what you're talking about. I wouldn't even know where to begin."

"That's something we could decide together," Joshua said eagerly. "Of course, I have some ideas already, but if you didn't think they'd work we could think of others."

Smiling regretfully, she shook her head. "It really sounds as if it would be exciting, but maybe you should hire somebody experienced in work like this. I would hate to make a mess of it for you."

"I'm sure you'd never do that," he persisted, lifting the journal out of the box with gentle fingers. He put it aside, then took a small packet of letters from the box. "Here, have a look at these. My grandfather wrote them to my grandmother during the war before they were married. They're really very interesting."

Susan took the packet reluctantly, afraid she might tear the thin yellowing paper, but it was impossible to resist untying the faded scarlet ribbon that held the letters together.

"Go ahead, read some of them," Joshua urged. "The ink is fading, but you've got better eyesight than me and I'm still able to make out the words."

Finally her curiosity overwhelmed her caution and she unfolded the first letter in the stack. And within a minute she was engrossed in the contents. A gripping loneliness was conveyed in the words of the nineteen-year-old soldier, away from home for the first time, and, as Susan read, it was almost as if she were with him when he realized that more than half his company had been killed or badly wounded at Antietam. His confusion and poignantly expressed desire to come home brought tears to her eyes, and suddenly Benjamin Thornton became a real person to her, a person she wanted to learn more about.

Obviously recognizing her reaction, Joshua patted her hand. "Here, read this one," he urged, extracting a letter from the middle of the packet. "He scribbled it down during the night before the second day of the Battle of Gettysburg. It's pretty obvious he didn't think he'd get out of Pennsylvania alive—and I guess it's a miracle he did, since he was one of the fifteen thousand in Pickett's charge on Cemetery Ridge."

"But he *did* survive the entire war, since you said he wasn't married to your grandmother yet when he wrote these letters."

"Oh, yes, he survived—lived to be a very old man, in fact, and he kept this journal for forty-two years." Joshua laughed. "He apparently had an ear for gossip, because he seemed to know everything about everybody in the county." He snapped his fingers suddenly. "Why, I bet you'd like to see my old picture album! There's a tintype of my grandfather and grandmother, made about a year after they got married." Standing, he lifted his eyebrows questioningly. "You would like to see it, wouldn't you? You are interested?" Then, when she assured him she was very interested, he grinned smugly. "You see, you'd probably enjoy helping me with my family's history."

"Oh, I'm sure I would, but I wonder exactly how much help I'd be. As I said, I've never tried to do anything like that."

"I'll get the album," he said anyway, walking across the room to the oak secretary again.

He certainly was persistent, Susan thought, smiling to herself as she watched him. And it certainly was pleasant to be treated as if she had something of value to offer someone. She glanced around the room. This would be a lovely place to work, and Mr. Thornton was an extremely agreeable man. And the project he was proposing did sound intriguing. It would be a challenge to take all this material and organize it. Maybe she should give his offer more serious consideration, she thought as he brought the album back to her.

The tintype of Benjamin and his wife, Margaret, was in surprisingly good condition. He was sitting stiffly in a large wicker chair while she stood behind him to one side, her hand resting on his shoulder. Neither of them wore even a hint of a smile, but there was still no denying that both of them had been attractive young people. Both had light hair and clean-cut features, and as Susan examined the picture carefully she felt a nagging sense of recognition, though she could not imagine why she should.

"Back here is a picture of my mother holding me when I was about four weeks old," Joshua said, flipping the stiff, thick pages. Then, as she admired his first photograph, he looked up as the sitting-room door was opened and someone came in.

"So you did decide to come," he said enthusiastically, waving the newcomer in. "I'm really glad you did. I wanted you to meet my new friend here."

As Joshua took her hand and patted it affectionately, Susan smiled and she turned toward the door. But her smile froze stiffly on her lips for a second before vanishing with her swift intake of breath. Standing in the doorway, staring malevolently at her, was the man she had hoped never to see again—her very own big jerk, Adam Kincaid.

Chapter Three

Susan shifted nervously on the sofa as Emily served pecan pie and coffee for dessert. She wouldn't be able to eat a morsel, she knew, not with Adam Kincaid sitting no more than two feet away from her, stroking his cheek with one long brown finger, eyeing her as if he were plotting the perfect murder.

Luckily, Joshua Thornton had not seemed to notice anything amiss when he had introduced her to his nephew, yet Susan was amazed that he had not. Shocked to silence by seeing *him* appear out of nowhere, she had only managed to move her mouth in a mute greeting as he had sauntered into the room to take the chair nearest her. Strangely enough, though, he had not seemed to share her surprise. With baffling calm, he had stretched his long legs out in front of him and leaned back in his chair as he chatted for a moment with his uncle.

Even now, as he declined the pie Emily offered but accepted the coffee, he was laughing easily at something the housekeeper said. It was only when he looked in Susan's direction again that he showed any sign that this was not a typical relaxing evening with his uncle, and that was evident only by a barely discernible tightening of his jaw and a narrowing of his green eyes.

Swallowing with difficulty, Susan looked away, her

hand shaking so violently that coffee from her cup
sloshed out onto the saucer she held. Groaning inwardly, she hastily set the saucer down on the table beside
her, next to the untouched slice of pie, then twisted her
hands together in her lap to control their trembling.

This simply was not fair, she thought as, out of the
corner of her eye, she watched Adam lazily light a
cigarette. After all the rotten things that had happened
to her today, this should not be happening now, just
when she was beginning to feel a little less like a failure.
But it *was* happening, and there was not anything she
could do except endure the time until she could ask that
Baker drive her home. Unless she pretended to be
suddenly overcome with a violent headache . . . No,
she couldn't do something so cowardly. Besides, such a
weak, unoriginal excuse would not convince either
Adam Kincaid or his uncle, and she would not want to
hurt Joshua's feelings by telling such a lie. Not that it
would be a lie if she had to sit here much longer.
Already a dull ache had begun to radiate from the back
of her head.

Unable to pay any attention to what Joshua and his
nephew were discussing, she sat very still, staring at her
hands in her lap until it finally occurred to her that she
was being spoken to.

"Pardon?" she said weakly, looking over at Joshua.
"I'm afraid I didn't hear what you said."

"Oh, it wasn't important. I was just making a little
joke. I asked if the cat had gotten your tongue." When
she forced a wan little smile, he continued: "I was just
telling Adam here that you might be coming to work
for me soon."

"And I was just about to ask my uncle what qualified
you to attempt such a complex undertaking," Adam
added, a hint of sarcasm in his voice as he shifted his
position in his chair. "Would you mind telling me what
some of those qualifications are?"

Since he had spoken to her directly, Susan had no choice except to look at him. But she drew back with a soft gasp when she saw that he was now leaning forward, resting his elbows on his knees so that his face was on a level with hers and much too disconcertingly close.

"My qualifications . . . Well, actually, I've never done anything like what your uncle is—"

"No, I thought not," Adam said smugly.

"But she studied journalism in college," Joshua protested. "And she's been working on a small newspaper for about a year, until just recently."

"Is that the truth?" Adam asked sharply, his expression indicating he doubted very much that it was. "Where did you go to school?"

"I studied one year at a very small college in South Carolina and another year and a half here."

"In Atlanta?"

"Well, no. Albany State."

"Why didn't you finish?"

He was beginning to irritate her again and Susan lifted her chin defiantly. "I was getting tired of going to school, and when I got a chance to work on the newspaper in my hometown I took it."

"So, you see, I think she's qualified," Joshua interceded then, perhaps detecting the impatience of her tone. "She's certainly had experience doing research, and I'm going to need help getting background material. That can be a very tiring job."

"But Miss Thomas undoubtedly came to Atlanta seeking a more exciting line of work, Uncle Josh. Why should she want to get involved in something like this?"

"I happen to think compiling a history of your uncle's family would be very exciting, Mr. Kincaid." Susan said stiffly. "He, and you, of course, have some very interesting ancestors."

"You really think so?" he asked, smiling disbelievingly. "But surely you're not trying to tell me you came all the way to Atlanta hoping to find someone who could use your services writing a family history."

"Why should I try to tell you that when it obviously couldn't be true?"

"But, Adam, since she can't find the exact job she wants, it seems to me this would be a very suitable temporary position," Joshua offered, frowning bewilderedly at their unfriendly exchange. "And I know I'll never be able to do this history at all without help."

"I realize that, Uncle Josh, but—"

"You *are* interested in doing it, aren't you, Susan?" Mr. Thornton asked her hopefully. "I know it would only be temporary, but I think it would be a great experience for you."

"So do I, and I've decided to accept your offer," Susan said abruptly, surprising herself with the realization that she was truly excited by the prospect of helping Joshua with his history. She did not regret accepting his offer so impetuously, especially when she met Adam Kincaid's threatening gaze. It was almost a perverse pleasure knowing she could be the source of such aggravation.

That pleasure faded within a few minutes, however, when Joshua decided she should move out to Maiden's Bower while they were doing their work. Then Adam's displeasure seemed to become almost tangible. After glaring at Susan as if she had been the originator of the idea, he sank back in his chair, his expression brooding as he lit another cigarette.

"I don't see why it would be necessary for Miss Thomas to move out here, Uncle Josh. Don't you think it would be better if Baker just went into town to get her every day?"

"I just think it would be more convenient for everybody if she stayed here."

"But maybe she wouldn't want to be so far from town. I'm sure Miss Thomas has quite a social life."

"What about that, Susan? Wouldn't it suit you to move in out here while we work?"

Before she could prevent herself, Susan glanced warily at Adam, who was staring at her, his glittering eyes conveying the message that he would make her extremely sorry if she accepted his uncle's hospitality. But she was feeling almost recklessly defiant tonight, and, since she realized she could not live with Barbara indefinitely, Joshua's offer was a temptation. The idea of living out here in this lovely old house among the trees appealed to her romantic nature. Besides, if she and Joshua agreed that she should move out here, what business was it of Adam Kincaid's anyway? It wasn't *any* of his business, she told herself, dragging her gaze away from his tanned face.

She smiled at Joshua. "I think you're probably right," she told him. "It might be more convenient for everyone if I just moved in." But as she heard Adam mutter something she felt sure was uncomplimentary behind her, most of her bravado deserted her. With a nervous gesture, she looked at her wristwatch. "Oh, my, I didn't realize it was so late. Do you think Baker could drive me back into town now?"

Even as Joshua Thornton nodded, Adam spoke up. "No need to bother Fred, Uncle Josh. I'd be happy to take Miss Thomas by her place on my way home."

When he stood then and actually reached down as if to help Susan up, she shrank back against the sofa cushions behind her, her eyes wide with apprehension. It was a reaction even Joshua could not fail to notice. Chuckling softly, he shook his head. "You needn't look so appalled, my dear," he said indulgently. "You can trust my nephew. He's a gentleman."

Biting back a disbelieving retort, she frowned at the sight of the satisfied little smile that was curving Adam's lips. He was actually relishing the fact that she was frightened of him. Determined to prove the contrary to him and to herself, she held out her hand, refusing to tremble when his lean, strong fingers closed tightly around it. But when he pulled her up to stand close before him, she wished his height were not quite so intimidating. Though she was not really short, five foot four, her eyes were only on the level of the third button down on his shirt, and it was rather disconcerting having to tilt her head back to look up at him. Sidestepping, she moved around him, but he was not so easily defeated. With an almost proprietary gesture, he placed his hand against the small of her back as they followed his uncle into the hall.

"Do you think you could be ready to move in by tomorrow afternoon?" Joshua asked hopefully as he took her jacket from the closet by the front door. "Would you like me to send Emily over to help you pack?"

"Oh, heavens, no, I don't have that much to bring," Susan told him with a nervous little laugh. Then, to her relief, Adam had to take his hand away while his uncle helped her with her jacket. "It won't take me very long to get ready."

"Then I think I'll send Baker over to pick you up about one tomorrow afternoon."

When Susan nodded agreeably, Joshua winked at his nephew. "Didn't I tell you Susan is a very charming young lady? And wasn't I right about her eyes? Aren't they beautiful? Such an unusual color." He turned back to her. "I talked to Adam just after I called you tonight and told him all about our meeting this afternoon."

"Oh, really," Susan said inadequately.

"Yes, really," Adam answered almost mockingly, his gaze sweeping over her. "And I have to admit, Uncle Josh, it was your description of her eyes that brought me out here. It isn't every day you get a chance to see eyes 'the color of spring violets.' They're very noticeable, aren't they? Memorable, in fact."

So he had suspected who she was before he had come to Maiden's Bower tonight, Susan realized with a sudden lurching of her heart. That explained why he had not been surprised to see her, but it did not explain why he acted as if she were some kind of criminal. Surely what she had said to him this morning had not been that horrible, unless he was one of those men who felt threatened by even a little defiance, especially from a female. And if he was that protective of his macho image, what might he do to punish someone he felt had tarnished it? Susan did not know and had no desire to find out, but, unfortunately, she knew she had little choice in the matter.

Much too soon, it seemed, they were saying their final goodnights to Joshua Thornton and Adam was escorting her out into the moonlit night. Susan cast several cautious glances in his direction as he maneuvered the sports car easily along the winding drive out onto the narrow secondary road, but she made no attempt to start a conversation. Something in the strength of his hands as one gripped the wheel and the other operated the gearshift discouraged her from trying to be pleasant. It did cross her mind that perhaps she should apologize for overreacting this morning, but as she turned her head and opened her mouth to do so he looked toward her, and at the cynical twist of his lips the words died in her throat.

Slumping down in her seat, she pressed herself close to the door, staring out at the dark pines that edged the road. But when Adam inexplicably turned down a narrow dirt lane, the swaying trees closing in on them from each side became menacing suddenly and claustrophobic. Straightening, she looked around quickly, hoping to see some sign that this route was a shortcut to the interstate, but apparently it was not. When the road ended abruptly at the edge of a wide, lonesome field, he stopped and cut the engine. An ominous silence engulfed Susan, constricting her breathing as she looked out blindly at the field of Johnson grass rippling in the brisk breeze in the pale moonlight. Then she jerked around, uttering a little cry of protest as Adam suddenly leaned toward her and reached out without ceremony to pull the pins from the loose chignon on her nape.

"Ah, that's better," he whispered as her dark, heavy hair tumbled down over the hand that gently clasped the back of her neck. "You look much freer this way."

"What are you doing?" she exclaimed breathlessly, her eyes wide as they searched his face. "Why have you brought me way out here?"

"Why do you think?" he murmured, rubbing one fingertip slowly across her lips until they parted with a soft, surprised gasp. "If you'll go so far as to chase after my uncle in the hope that I'll give you a modeling job, it's obvious you'd be willing to do a lot more. But I don't like to rush these things too much. Preliminaries make it all the more exciting, don't you agree? An hour or so here will heighten the anticipation considerably before we go to my place."

"What are you talking about? Why are you doing this?" she cried, pushing his hand away from her mouth, twisting her head in an effort to loosen his grip on her neck. But her struggles ceased immediately as his fingers entwined in her hair, causing considerable pain. "Don't, please," she whispered urgently. "You've gotten the wrong idea s-somehow. I don't . . . I just couldn't . . ."

"Then stop acting as if you'd do anything to get a job modeling, you little idiot!" he said harshly, releasing her hair only to grasp her chin in hard, cruel fingers. "Using my uncle to try to get close to me is a pretty desperate ploy, one that indicates you'd also be willing, as some girls are, to trade sex for a modeling assignment. But you're not willing! And I've scared you now, I hope. You know, you're very lucky you tried this little trick with me. Some men wouldn't realize how obviously inexperienced you are, and even if they did they might expect you to come through, scared or not."

Susan glared at him, outraged by his ridiculous accusation. "You really are crazy! And conceited too! I'm not using your uncle to try to get close to you, because I don't want a modeling job. And, besides, if I'm so obviously inexperienced why on earth do you think I'd ever encourage . . . that I'd pretend to be willing to . . . to . . ."

He smiled mockingly. "You see, you little simpleton, you can't even bring yourself to say it. So you'd better watch out—don't give the impression that you're desperate enough to sleep around to get a job."

Her mouth fell open for a second before she snapped it shut.

"You think I . . . You are incredible! I've never met anybody who could jump to the wrong conclusions the way you can! I told you this morning I'm not the least bit interested in anything you have."

"Of course you're not," he retorted sarcastically. "Then why are you trying to get in good with my uncle? I suppose you'll try to tell me that you simply like him? And I guess you want me to believe seeing me with him in the park today had nothing to do with your approaching him after I left?"

For a moment Susan could only mutter with incoherent fury, but finally she managed to control her anger enough to make some sense.

"Contrary to what you believe, Mr. Kincaid, my world does not revolve around you," she said tersely, her eyes flashing. "I didn't even know you were in the park today, much less see you talking to Mr. Thornton. The only reason I approached him at all was that I could see he wasn't feeling well and it looked as if he could use some help. We had a nice little chat, then said good-bye, and I didn't think I'd ever see him again. But when he called tonight and said he had some information about a job for me, naturally I was interested since I haven't been having much luck getting one on my own. I had no idea he would offer me a job working for

him, but now that he has I'm very excited about it.
Now, that's all there is to it. If you don't believe me,
I'm—"

"You're either very naïve or very stupid if you think
I'll believe a line like that," Adam said disgustedly.
"This morning you were begging for a chance to do
some modeling, but tonight you try to tell me you're
very excited about helping Uncle Josh with a family
history that could not possibly interest you in the
least."

"But you're all wrong about this mor—"

"I want you to call my uncle first thing in the morning
and tell him you've changed your mind," he interrupted imperiously. "I want this thing stopped before it
has a chance to begin."

"I'll do no such thing! I need that job, and your uncle
needs my help! You can't tell me what to do! What right
do you have to interfere in—"

"I have every right," Adam said through clenched
teeth, reaching out to grasp her upper arms. "My
uncle's not a well man, and I won't allow anybody to
upset him. I'm not about to let you get his hopes up
about this history, then disappoint him in a couple of
weeks when you walk out on him because you've found
a job more to your liking."

"But I'd never do that to him! What do you think I
am?"

"I think you're a silly little girl who decided to come
to Atlanta and make it big as a model. Unfortunately,
you didn't realize it would take a little longer than two
weeks, and now you're getting desperate. So you
decided to push your way into the business, even if you
had to use a lonely old man to do it, even if you had to
sleep around to do it. You're just lucky you tried this
approach with me and not some of my associates. *I*
have a policy against taking innocent little girls to bed."

"Why? Because they aren't as much fun as someone
experienced?" Susan retorted, blushing as she realized

how crude her words sounded and wishing she could recall them as he grinned.

"That's part of the reason, yes. But mostly I have no desire to take on the awesome responsibility of being a young woman's first lover. I'd hate her to get the idea I should make an honest woman out of her again by marrying her."

"You're completely obnoxious," she muttered furiously, trying with little success to pry his fingers from around her arms. "And I can tell you right now, you'd never have to worry about me wanting to marry you! I wouldn't have you even if you—"

"Even if I did become your first lover?" he murmured provocatively, pulling her to him without regard for the gear console. Turning her so that only her legs lay across it, cradling her in his strong arms, he lowered his head to kiss her.

Knowing this was only part of his attempt to humiliate her, Susan refused to panic and held herself stiffly even as he gathered her much closer so that the softness of her body yielded to the firm line of his chest. But as he brushed his firm mouth slowly back and forth over her tightly closed lips, the intimate touch sent a shaft of awareness through her like an unexpected electric shock. With a soft moan her mouth opened eagerly beneath his, and she found herself unable to resist the compelling hardness of the lips that took hers with little gentleness. Now it no longer seemed to matter why he was kissing her. All that she cared about was that he continue. Somehow her hand slid into his shirt next to his heated flesh. Her fingers began stroking the taut muscles of his chest while his mouth sought the tantalizingly scented skin of her slender neck. His hands encircled her waist roughly while his thumbs brushed caressingly over the firm curves of her breasts.

"No," she felt compelled to whisper. "Don't do that."

But he did not stop. "What do you expect after being

so responsive?" he said huskily into her ear. "You certainly believe in living dangerously, don't you? You could make me change my policy about inexperienced girls."

"Oh, just stop trying to frighten me," she muttered and pushed herself away from him to settle back in her own seat. As she tugged her skirt down over her knees, she tried to overcome the incongruous disappointment she felt that what had just happened had only been part of his plan to intimidate her. "I'm not sixteen years old, you know. I'm twenty-one, and your threats don't scare me."

"Then why are you way over there?" he asked with an amused chuckle as he lit a cigarette. When she shrank away from the touch of his fingers on her shoulder as he draped his arm over the back of her seat, he shook his head. "You've gotten in over your head, haven't you? And now you're not exactly sure how to get out gracefully."

"I can take care of myself just fine, thank you."

"The safest answer for you is to call Uncle Josh tomorrow and tell him you've had second thoughts."

"But I don't intend to do that, and you can't make me."

Grasping a strand of her tousled hair, he forced her to turn her head and face him. "All right, maybe I can't make you change your mind. But I'm warning you right now, if you try to walk out on him before this project's completed to his satisfaction, I'll forget how inexperienced you are and see that we finish what we started tonight."

"Hah! That doesn't scare me in the least. Even *you* wouldn't resort to rape."

"But I wouldn't have to, would I?" he whispered, smiling slightly when the touch of his fingertip on her lips made her tremble. "You weren't faking that response a moment ago. I know it and, more important, you know it."

"What nonsense," she uttered weakly, unwilling to consider even for a second that what he was saying might be true. Pushing his hand away, she turned her head again to stare unseeingly out the window. "I'm not going to walk out on your uncle anyway, so your threats aren't necessary."

"I hope not," Adam answered, his tone seriously concerned. "I think you should know Uncle Josh is a very lonely man and you're not the first girl he's brought home with him."

Her eyes widened in astonishment as they darted to his face. "What are you saying? You mean he picks up girls for . . . for . . ."

"Oh, of course not!" Adam snapped impatiently. "I can assure you Uncle Josh has no designs on you physically. But he's likely to become very attached to you, and I don't want you treating him the way the others did. Both of them just up and left—and the last one took along two thousand dollars from his safe on her way out the door."

"Oh, no! How could she do that to such a sweet old gentleman? How awful for him!"

"Luckily, he never knew she did it. Baker found the safe open and saw the money was missing. He called me and I took two thousand dollars out there to replace it. We couldn't let him discover what she'd done because, despite the fact that she wasn't really a very nice young lady, he had grown fond of her. Frankly, his heart's not in very good shape, and I was afraid the shock of learning she was a common thief would bring on an attack. Now maybe you can understand why I'll make you very sorry if you do anything at all to upset him."

"But *I* am not a thief, Mr. Kincaid," Susan said icily. "So you don't have to worry that I might run off with the family jewels."

"I never imagined you would," he admitted surprisingly. "I just want to be sure you know exactly how vulnerable Uncle Josh is. Aunt Meredith died two years ago and he's been lost without her. They were extremely close, especially after my cousin, Catherine, died nineteen years ago when she was twenty. So, you see, girls your age mean something very special to him."

"He never even mentioned a daughter to me," Susan said sadly. "He didn't say a word."

"He's never talked about it much. I always thought he had taken her death extremely well, but obviously he still misses her or he wouldn't look to young women for companionship."

"Well, I can assure you I'll never do anything to hurt him."

Adam eyed her skeptically.

"Not even if a nice little modeling job came along in a couple of weeks? Come on, now, you know you'd feel you had to take it."

"But one's not likely to come along, is it?" she asked resentfully, suddenly reminded of all the uncomplimentary remarks he had made that morning. "After all, you told me yourself that I'm not tall enough or sophisticated enough or pretty enough to ever be a model. So I can't see what you're worrying about anyway, since I'm such a total wreck."

His dark green eyes traveled slowly over her, lingering for a long, intense moment on her mouth, and the smile he gave her was almost teasing.

"You *are* very young, aren't you?" he asked gently, lifting a silencing hand at her attempted protest. "I remember exactly what I said to you today, and I definitely did not tell you that you aren't pretty."

"Well, you made me *feel* unattractive," Susan muttered rather petulantly. "I'd had an awful morning. You should try to remember people do have feelings. You didn't need to be so honest about what's wrong with how I look."

"I repeat again—there's nothing wrong with how you look."

Shaking her head almost childishly, she stared un-willingly at his brown hand resting with latent strength against his hard, muscular thigh. Chewing her lip, she watched that his hand reached out slowly to cover her own. Then her reproachful eyes lifted to meet the enigmatic darkening in his.

"How can you believe I don't think you're attractive after what happened between us a few minutes ago?" he asked in a whisper. "Surely my response to you showed you quite clearly that I find you very attractive."

"You don't have to pretend," she whispered back chidingly. "I know what you were doing—you were just trying to frighten me out of working for your uncle."

"And did I? Frighten you, I mean? Aren't you afraid I'll make good my threats?" When she shook her head, his eyes narrowed and he lifted her hand to his mouth, pressing his warm, firm lips against her palm, holding her gaze. "So you think you can trust me not to try to seduce you?"

Susan nodded again, willing her fingers not to brush his cheek caressingly. "Why shouldn't I trust you?" she murmured a little breathlessly. "You said inexperi-enced girls aren't enough fun."

"So I did," he answered, dropping her hand to swing around and turn the key in the ignition. As the engine roared to life, he gripped the steering wheel with both hands, then looked at her once again. "Keep trusting me, Susan," he whispered cryptically. "That may be the only chance you have."

Chapter Four

Joshua patted the cushion next to him on the brown leather sofa.

"Come on, sit down awhile," he coaxed. "You're making me feel mighty guilty for just sitting here while you climb up and down and do all the work."

Rolling aside the ladder that enabled her to reach the ceiling-high bookshelves, Susan smiled at her employer and tucked a wayward strand of hair behind her ear as she walked across the library to join him.

"How about some refreshment?" she asked him before she sat down. "I'll go tell Emily you'd like some tea if you want me to. And I think she made some cookies this morning; a few of those might be good."

"Stop trying to coddle me," he admonished good-naturedly as he shook his head. "I'm not hungry, but if you'd like something . . ."

"No, I just thought you might since you ate very little lunch."

"I bet it's that Emily who's got you spying on me, isn't it? Or is it Adam? Both of them act like I'm a little baby that has to be watched every minute. They forget I've been looking after myself for a good many years now."

"Oh, you know they only worry about you because they love you," Susan said as she sat down beside him after brushing from her wine-colored skirt a bit of dust that had come off the top-shelf books she had taken down. "Now, you'd have real reason to complain if they didn't care whether you ate or not."

And when Joshua smiled to himself and nodded, she watched him. He was a dear man, and in the two weeks she had been at Maiden's Bower she had become very fond of him. He was never querulous and short-tempered as her own grandparents were sometimes. But, in all fairness, her grandparents had to contend with six grandchildren, all of whom lived within walking distance of their house, while Joshua had no one to bestow his love on except Adam, Emily and Fred Baker, and now Susan herself.

"Are you happy here, honey?" he asked abruptly and with a certain urgency. "I imagine you must be a little disappointed that I'm not up to going great guns on this history. It makes it less exciting, doesn't it, when you have to just plod along?"

"But I don't feel that we're just plodding along," she assured him hastily. "We've decided how everything's going to be arranged, and in a few days you'll have dictated all the prologue to me."

"That's turning out better than I ever thought it would," Joshua agreed enthusiastically. "Sometimes those things can bore a reader to tears, but at least old Great-grandfather Jonathan had some adventures before he decided to settle down."

"Yes. Stowing away on a ship to get here does start things off with a bang."

Joshua chuckled, glancing at her mischievously. "I guess old Jonathan never was one to let the grass grow under his feet. He was quite the ladies' man for a lot of years until Felicity Hooper grew up and caught his fancy. And even then he didn't give up his wild ways easily—instead of making things simple for everybody by marrying her, he had to seduce her first." Leaning closer, he whispered with mock indignation: "Felicity

was already in the family way on their wedding day,
you know."

"So I'd gathered," Susan responded with a grin.
"Isn't that disgraceful?"

"Shocking," he agreed, fighting a smile. "I have to
admit that several other of the men in my family were
rather wild, but only before they got married, of
course. After that, they became exemplary husbands
and fathers."

"Are you including yourself in that list?"

Joshua smiled a little sheepishly as he shrugged. "I
guess you could say I had my moments, but only until I
met Meredith. Other women didn't interest me after
that." Smiling reminiscently, he stared off into space
for several seconds, then sighed. "I keep waiting for
Adam to find a young lady to settle him down. He's
already thirty-four years old—I was a father by that
age. But I guess he'll really fall in love sooner or later
and stop all this running around."

Don't count on that, she wanted to say but did not,
knowing that Joshua would then ask her why she felt
that his nephew would never be a willing family man.
She had no desire to reveal the events that had given
her that impression, since the memory of his actions
and her subsequent response disturbed her more than
enough already. It was better not to think about Adam
Kincaid at all; but, though she tried her best to push
him from her mind, it was not always an easy accomplishment, especially when he came to Maiden's
Bower. And he came often—checking up on her, she
supposed, since Joshua had mentioned that his visits
were more frequent lately.

If only she could convince him to trust her with his
uncle, she thought with an involuntary sigh, everything
would be much more pleasant for her and infinitely
more relaxed. It was not particularly soothing to know
that Adam was always watching her closely when he
was here, as if he fully expected her to pounce on poor

Joshua at any minute. Every hour he spent here was a tense ordeal that made her unusually self-conscious—and sometimes angry when it seemed obvious that he found her nervousness amusing. Often, when she would look at him, she would catch a hint of a smug smile hovering on his lips and she would long to slap his face for entertaining himself at her expense.

Yet even more disturbing were the moments when she glanced up to find him watching her with an altogether different expression, an expression she could not identify. Then his narrowed dark eyes would move over her with such slow, intense appraisal that her cheeks would burn hotly and she would press herself into her chair, trying to make herself smaller and less noticeable. Finally, when she could stand it no longer, she would meet his eyes directly, breathing a sigh of relief when he would rouse himself from whatever dark, unpleasant thoughts he was having.

Luckily for her, Joshua attributed her tenseness around his nephew to simple shyness, and if he ever wondered if perhaps there was a deeper reason for their wary attitude toward each other he never questioned her about it and she never enlightened him. It was much easier to laugh off his teasing remarks concerning her shyness around older men than it ever would have been to try to admit to him that it was not all older men who reduced her to quiet self-consciousness; it was only Adam who had such an ability. Why couldn't it have been different, she wondered a little sadly. Adam could be a very personable man, quite magnetic actually, and she often wished their first meeting had not been such a total disaster. But it had been, and since it was impossible to change the past she knew she might as well accept the situation exactly as it was, without allowing herself to brood about how much more pleasant it could have been.

As she sat staring at her fingernails, she sighed again, then glanced warily at Joshua, hoping he would not question that sigh. But he was resting his head back against the wing of the sofa, apparently asleep.

Getting up very quietly, she tiptoed across the room to the desk, where she sat down and began going through the notes she had made that morning. As she arranged several events in Jonathan Thornton's life chronologically, she looked up occasionally to check on Joshua. She worried about him. Since her very first day here she had realized he really was not well enough to attempt this history of his family, but he was so determined to do it that she hadn't tried to dissuade him. Instead, she simply made certain that he did not overexert himself; but even then he tired easily and, as often as not, she found herself working alone some of the mornings and all of the afternoons while he dozed on the sofa. It was his history, though, and she had no intentions of taking it over completely. He made all the major decisions and she was quite content with that arrangement. It was enough for her to be involved in compiling a family history that would ultimately read more like a novel because the Thorntons had not led dull lives. She was especially intrigued with Joshua's stories about Jonathan. At night, when she lay in bed listening to the bare branches of the trees rattling in the wind, she would try to imagine how the reckless Felicity had felt coming into this house as a bride, considering the circumstances surrounding her marriage to Jonathan. She must have wondered why he had changed his mind and decided to marry her after initially choosing to duel her father rather than to make her his wife. She must have felt so alone—disowned by her family, ostracized by the few neighbors, and always having to wonder if the man she obviously loved very much had only married her because she was carrying his child.

Unfortunately, the truth about the early days could never be known for certain. Felicity had never kept a diary, and Jonathan's began some five years into their marriage. He had fallen in love with her by then; the tenderness with which he wrote about her made that very plain. Yet Susan still could not shake the strong feeling that he had been rather cruel in the beginning.

Maybe she was not being completely fair, she considered as she sorted a stack of index cards. Somehow, in her mind she had identified Jonathan Thornton with Adam Kincaid, and that could account for her feeling the way she did. She could not see Adam being especially kind to any girl who made him sacrifice his freedom.

"You're getting too involved," she muttered to herself as she straightened a stack of papers on the desk. Then the phone suddenly rang, and she snatched up the receiver, hoping the abbreviated ring had not awakened Joshua. It had, however, and the sight of his sleepy, questioning face did not make her feel any too gracious, especially when the caller identified herself as Nellie Brooks and demanded to speak with him.

Susan forced herself to be at least polite. "I'm sorry, Miss Brooks, Mr. Thornton is resting right now and I can't disturb him. I'd be glad to give him a message for you, though, or have him call you back later."

"I'd really prefer talking to him personally and right now, if that's at all possible. I have something very important to discuss with him."

"I really can't disturb him. I'm sorry, but I promise I'll have him call you back as—"

"No. I can't wait around here for him to call me. I have much too much to do. You just give him a message. Tell him I'm bringing a couple of models and photographers to shoot the artwork for a magazine ad. The grounds are the perfect setting."

"Don't you think you should talk to him about this first? I don't think you should just come without arranging it all with him."

"With whom am I speaking?" Nellie asked icily. "You don't happen to be the girl who caused all the trouble at the studio a couple of weeks ago, do you?"

"Well, I—"

"Of course you are. Adam told me his uncle had hired you for something. What was it now? Oh, yes!" Nellie exclaimed with an infuriatingly unpleasant laugh. "I remember now. You're supposed to be helping him write up his family history, aren't you? Adam said it was going to be quite a project. So how's it going?"

"Fine," Susan murmured, wondering what else Adam had told her. "Now, do you want me to have Mr. Thornton call you back about your request to use the grounds?"

"No, I don't want him to call me back," Nellie replied. "I told you once I don't have time to wait for a return call. And it wouldn't be necessary anyway. Just tell him I'm bringing some people out early in the morning."

"But, Miss Brooks, you can't—"

"Oh, but I can. Adam's already told me he knows his uncle won't mind, and I've gone ahead and made all the arrangements."

"Oh, I see."

"Yes, I imagine you do—finally. Now, can you remember to give Mr. Thornton that message?"

"Well, if you have twenty minutes and wouldn't mind very much spelling it all out to me, I think I can manage to write it down," Susan retorted with equal sarcasm. "Hold on a second, though, while I get my big Mickey Mouse pencil." Though her mocking humor was rewarded with a snort of disgust and a loud bang as the receiver was slammed down in her ear, she was smiling with satisfaction as she got up from the desk.

"What was that all about?" Joshua asked her as she walked across the room. "It didn't sound very friendly."

"It wasn't. I'm afraid friendly is something Nellie Brooks and I will never be."

"Ah, so the formidable Nellie strikes again, eh?" he said with an understanding nod. "Not the warmest young lady in the world, is she? What reason did she have for calling here?"

"She wanted to inform you that early tomorrow morning she'll be arriving here with a couple of models and photographers. She plans to use your grounds as the setting for the artwork of some magazine ad she's doing."

"Oh no she isn't!" Joshua said with uncharacteristic vehemence. "She won't be doing anything here unless she asks my permission first."

"I told her I thought she should talk to you about it first, but she said Adam had told her he was sure you wouldn't mind."

"Really? How odd," Joshua said, frowning perplexedly. "That doesn't sound like something he would do without discussing it with me. Ah, well, he must have just forgotten to mention it." He gestured resignedly. "But if he told her it was all right, I guess I can't do much about it now. If the client has already approved the comprehensives, I'd better not do anything to upset the apple cart."

Susan was frowning too now as she tapped her forefinger against her cheek. "I thought Nellie's job was to buy ad space in magazines and newspapers. Why should she have to be here when they're doing the photography?"

"Adam told me she's been hounding him for months to get her out of the media department, so when he had an opening upstairs he decided to let her give it a try." Shaking his head, he smiled rather grimly. "If my old partner Nathan Simpson knew she'd invaded the executive offices, he'd probably sell his house in the West Indies and come out of retirement just so he could throw her out."

"Oh, is he a male chauvinist?"

"Probably," Joshua admitted with a wry grin. "But mostly he just wouldn't like Nellie."

Susan had to laugh. But her amusement did not

last very long as she realized she would probably have to put up with Nellie Brooks for several hours tomorrow.

Nellie and her entourage descended on the house before seven the next morning, before either Susan or Joshua had even gone downstairs for breakfast. And the "couple of models and photographers" turned out to be about a dozen girls and nearly half as many photographers plus their assistants. And all of them dragged their various paraphernalia into the front hall and plopped it down with little regard for the gleaming hardwood floors.

When Susan came down the stairs a few minutes after their arrival, she stopped and stared disbelievingly at the jumble of tote bags, camera cases, tripods, and discarded coats that littered the floor. There was not a soul to be seen anywhere, however, and for a moment Susan could not imagine where the people who owned this mess could possibly be. Then she heard a burst of laughter coming from the dining room. Before she could get down the hall to see what was happening, Emily came stamping out of the room, glaring back over her shoulder several times as she rushed toward the kitchen at the back of the house.

"Wait," Susan called after her as she ran to catch up. She tilted her head toward the dining room. "What's going on in there, Emily?" she asked in a whisper.

"That's exactly what I'd like to know," the housekeeper whispered back furiously, slapping a strand of gray hair back from her face. "Mr. Joshua didn't say nothing last night about me having to fix for them folks. He just said five or six people was going to be messing out on the grounds." She gestured impatiently. "Heaven have mercy, Miss Thomas, there must be twenty-five people in that dining room."

"I know I didn't misunderstand her," Susan murmured, mostly to herself, as she gazed at the floor.

Then she looked up again. "What are they doing in there?"

"They want coffee," Emily told her indignantly. "That woman that's running things just walked right in the door and told me to show them the dining room, then get them all some coffee. Now, I like to have some warning about these things, Miss Thomas. I'm going to have to go hunt up Fred and get him to get a bunch of cups down for me. You see, I could have had him do that last night if somebody had told me there'd be so many coming."

"Well, just go on and do what you can without rushing around," Susan told her. "Miss Brooks will just have to wait awhile for her coffee."

"Hmmph, I reckon she will," Emily said, fuming on as she went down the hall.

As Susan watched her go, she sighed as she realized she had better go warn Joshua. But she was too late. As she lifted her foot to the first step, she saw him at the top of the stairs.

"What is all that junk in my hall?" he boomed out, his face flushing a frightening red.

Susan sped up the steps to him, taking his arm, fearing his angry reaction might bring on a heart attack.

"Don't get too upset, now," she pleaded, leading him back toward his room despite his protest. "It's just Nellie and her gang. She obviously doesn't know that a couple usually means two."

"You mean to tell me that she's brought a busload of people out here?" Joshua grumbled, less loudly this time. "And she just invited them all into the house?"

"I'm afraid she did," Susan said as she gestured toward the easy chair next to his four-poster bed. "But I can take care of them. Why don't you sit here and relax while I go down and scoot them outside? Then we can get started in the library."

After he reluctantly agreed to that plan, Susan did go

downstairs, but it took nearly an hour to clear the dining room—and when Emily saw the overflowing ashtrays and dirty coffee cups the mob had left in its wake, there was another person to soothe. Finally, after helping carry the dirty dishes to the kitchen, she was able to get back to Joshua, who was in a very irritable frame of mind.

The next three hours did nothing to improve his mood. Though they closed themselves up in the library, every five minutes or so they heard the front door bang shut as three or four models came rushing in to go change their clothes upstairs in the bedroom that Nellie had commandeered for that purpose. Visibly tired yet unable to doze off because of the banging front door, Joshua got up to stare out the wide library windows.

"What the devil?" he exclaimed abruptly, gesturing urgently for Susan to come. And when she was beside him, he pointed out toward the gazebo. "Look at that fool woman! Do you see what she's doing? She's leading half that crowd right through Meredith's flower beds! By heaven, I'm putting a stop to this mess right this minute!"

"No, wait, please," Susan begged, catching his arm as he started to move away. "Let me go tell her to get out of the flowers—or I'll get Baker to go. You don't need to go out there and get yourself any more upset. *Please*. Meredith wouldn't have wanted you to make yourself ill just for her flower beds."

Suddenly Joshua relaxed and smiled down at her. "Why, you little vixen, you remind me of her in some ways—she always knew what to say to get me to do exactly what she wanted, just like you just did."

"Well, then, you sit down here and wait until I go tell Baker to run out there and chase Nellie out of the garden. Don't even worry about it anymore—I can handle it."

As he settled himself obediently on the sofa, he chuckled and shook his head. "You surprise me, little

Susan. You look very delicate but you can be tough when you have to, can't you?"

"Yes, I can be a real terror." Just ask your nephew, she added under her breath as she went out into the hall.

Terror or not, Susan found that Nellie Brooks was not very easy to control. Fred Baker's request that she move herself and everybody else from his iris beds was completely ignored, and he came, mumbling to himself, back into the kitchen where Susan waited.

"If that little girl was a daughter of mine, she'd find herself over my knee pretty quick," he grumbled angrily. "She's got a real sassy mouth."

"Did she get out of the garden, though?" Susan asked him.

"No, ma'am, she did not! Said they'd all get out as soon as they was finished taking all the shots they needed with that line of cedars as the background."

"But did you tell her Mr. Thornton was getting very upset because they were trampling through there?"

"I told her. And I told her it hadn't been long since I divided all the iris bulbs and replanted them right where they are setting up the cameras. But it didn't matter to her. She just said they weren't going to hurt my irises—but, let me tell you, it ain't going to do them no good to be walked all over that way."

"No, of course not," Susan murmured, wondering what to do now. She could not and would not go back into the library and tell Joshua that they couldn't pry Nellie out of garden. Without taking time to go upstairs for a sweater, she went out the back door across the browning lawn toward the gazebo. Falling leaves swirled down from the trees, dotting the lawn with oranges and yellows, and the breeze that carried them along was surprisingly cool. Susan hugged her arms across her chest as she went down the flagstone path into the large garden. Asters still bloomed in whites and yellows in one section, and they and the evergreen shrubbery provided enough color to make the gardens worth a visit even this late in the year. But, judging from the number of footprints Susan saw in the flower beds, there might not be much left to look at when Nellie got through.

No one even seemed to notice her as she approached the crowd. The photographers were too busy complaining about the legs of their tripods sinking into the soft, recently turned soil, and the models were listening with half interest to Nellie's instructions. Nellie herself continued issuing her orders and only glanced at Susan for a second before looking away again without acknowledging her presence.

Susan's patience was very nearly gone. With an impatient sigh, she grasped Nellie's arm and turned her around. "Look, Miss Brooks, whether you're finished shooting here or not, you *are* going to have to leave the garden. You've set up right in the middle of the iris bed, and Mr. Thornton won't allow you to do any more damage than you already have."

Nellie's thin arched brows lifted mockingly. "And why doesn't Mr. Thornton come tell me that himself? Does he even know we're out here, or did you just decide to tell us to leave on your own?"

"Mr. Thornton knows you're here and he's very upset," Susan told her, striving to control her temper. "This garden meant a lot to his wife, and he doesn't want to see it destroyed by you and your people. He was going to come out here and tell you to leave himself until I persuaded him to let me send Baker. He can't afford to get too upset, you see; he's not at all well."

Nellie waved her hand disparagingly. "Really, I can't see why he's getting all upset. We're not hurting a thing out here. There's not even anything growing."

"But the iris bulbs have just been replanted! You're walking all over them right now; that can't be doing them any good. It seems to me if Mr. Thornton was nice enough to let you use his grounds you could at least be considerate enough not to ruin his garden in the process."

"For heaven's sake, Nellie, let's just move someplace else," one of the photographers spoke up then. "There are a few cedars on the other side of the house. No use tramping through the garden if we don't have to."

"Do you mind staying out of this?" Nellie muttered heatedly, giving the man a withering glare. Then she turned back to Susan. "The cedars on the other side of the house are not as pretty as these, and now that we're all set up I see no reason to move."

"I think the fact that Mr. Thornton wants you to should be reason enough, even for someone as inconsiderate as you are!" Susan said, clenching her fists at her side. "And I think you'd better start moving your equipment right this minute."

"I don't care what you think!" Nellie shot back, raking her fingers through the short, feathery blonde hair that swept across her forehead. "I'm not going anywhere until Mr. Thornton himself asks me to move. And I don't think he will, because I don't think he cares that we're out here. I think you made the whole thing up so you could come out here and disrupt our work, just like you did that day at the studio."

For a moment Susan only stared at her incredulously; then, knowing it was useless to try to reason with her, she spun around and marched away, realizing there was only one option left.

"I'm calling Mr. Kincaid," she answered Fred and Emily Baker's questioning expressions as she came in through the kitchen door. "She won't move and I can't go in there and tell Mr. Thornton that. Emily, do you have a number where I can reach him?"

Emily did, and Susan used the phone in the kitchen to put the call through. She was put on hold for a few minutes, but when Adam finally came on the line she explained the trouble briefly after assuring him that his uncle was all right so far. Adam said he would be right out.

He must have broken the speed limit, for before Susan realized it he was there, striding into the library, a worried expression on his lean, tanned face.

"Are you sure you're all right, Uncle Josh?" was his first question. Then he turned to Susan. "Now, what exactly is all this about?"

She sank down on the edge of a brown leather chair. "You know, of course, that Miss Brooks is out here getting some pictures."

"She told me she was coming, yes."

"Well, yesterday, when she called here and said she'd be out today, she made it sound as if she were only bringing three or four other people; but this morning she showed up with about twenty, and they sort of invaded the house, upsetting Emily and—"

"And me," Joshua put in abruptly. "You should have seen the mess they made in the hall, and now they're out tearing up Meredith's garden!"

"Whoa, whoa, wait a minute," Adam said calmly, a puzzled frown creasing his brow as he looked at Susan. "Let's go back to the beginning for a second. What did you mean exactly when you said Nellie called and *said* she'd be out here today?"

"She just said she'd be here with a couple of models and photographers."

"And she didn't speak to you, Uncle Josh?"

"Well, no," Joshua answered, smiling rather sheepishly. "I had dozed off for a minute or two and I guess Susan didn't want to disturb me."

"No, I didn't. I did tell Miss Brooks I'd be happy to have him call her back, but she said it wasn't necessary. I was to simply tell him she would be coming out today."

Still watching Susan closely, Adam's green eyes narrowed.

She shifted nervously on the edge of the sofa, returning his stare with wide, uncertain eyes, wondering what she had done wrong this time. Then she breathed a sigh of relief as he suddenly raked his fingers through the thick silvery hair on the nape of his neck and gave her a slight yet seemingly sincere little smile. And when he held out one hand to her, she found herself immediately laying her own in it.

"I wonder if you would mind very much going out and telling Nellie I want to see her in here right away," he asked as he helped her up. "I'd like to talk to Uncle Josh for a moment or I'd go myself."

"I don't mind," she murmured, breathing a little more quickly than she should have been. But he was standing so close she could detect the strong beat of his pulse in his temples, and the clean masculine fragrance of his aftershave enveloped her, bringing back in a rush the memory of that night in his car and how she had felt when he kissed her. "I'll be right back," she whispered unevenly, backing away, not wanting to remember.

A minute later Susan found some satisfaction in the startled expression that fleetingly crossed Nellie's face when she heard that Adam was in the house and wanted to see her. But the older woman composed herself almost immediately and her face took on its old familiar look of haughty disdain. Then, without a word, she buttoned the jacket of her tweed suit over her blue silk blouse and marched away, leaving Susan to follow in the wake of expensive French perfume.

By the time she walked into the front hall, Nellie was swishing her way into the library, with an enthusiastic cry of welcome for Adam.

"Darling, I didn't expect to see you here today," she was saying as Susan came into the room. "I thought you had several clients to see."

"What's the problem out here, Nellie?" he began immediately, not even bothering to acknowledge her greeting. "Uncle Josh says he had no idea you planned to bring a whole mob of people with you today."

Without even blinking, Nellie turned to Susan. "Oh, did you forget to tell him, dear?" she asked, shaking her head indulgently as she turned back to Adam. "It slipped her mind, I suppose."

Shocked to silence by the woman's audacity, Susan could not speak. But Joshua had no such problem.

"She told me you were coming, Nellie," he said tersely. "But you told her you were bringing a couple of models and photographers, not half of Atlanta."

"Oh, but I'm sure I told her there would be quite a few of us," Nellie protested, giving him a supposedly apologetic smile. "She must have just misunderstood what I said."

Joshua gestured impatiently. "I doubt that. Susan rarely misunderstands anything I tell her."

Laughing lightly, Nellie tucked her hand into the crook of Adam's arm, a possessive gesture that did not seem to particularly please him. And she obviously did not see the tightening of his jaw as he looked down at her.

"Really, I don't see how everything could have gotten all mixed up this way unless Miss Thomas did misunderstand what I said. I did have some misgivings about leaving a message with her, but since she refused to let me talk to you, Mr. Thornton, I didn't have any other choice."

Adam intervened. "Didn't Susan offer to have Uncle Josh call you back, Nellie? And didn't you tell her that he didn't need to do that?"

"I don't recall her offering to have him return my call," Nellie lied with unbelievable ease. "She just said I couldn't talk to him."

Adam looked past her to Susan, who was still close by the door, staring at Nellie. "What do you have to say about that?" he asked grimly.

Shaking her head, Susan swallowed with difficulty, recognizing the no-nonsense tone of voice that had always meant trouble for her. "I did offer to have Mr. Thornton call her back," she said adamantly, not really expecting him to believe her. "I did."

"Of course she did!" Joshua exclaimed, struggling to his feet. "I might have been sleepy, but I know I heard her say she'd have me call you back, Nellie."

"Oh, were you in the room? Well, I guess I might just not have heard her, but if you were available, why did she refuse to let me speak with you?"

"Because I was resting! She never disturbs me when I'm resting!"

"Don't get so upset, Uncle Josh," Adam said worriedly. "We'll get all this straightened out." He removed Nellie's clinging fingers from his arm. "Now, what I want to know is why you never asked my uncle for permission to come out here. Why did you simply call and say you were coming?"

"She wouldn't let me talk to him!"

"Then you shouldn't have come," Adam said flatly. "Not without his okay."

"But *she* said it would be all right!"

"I certainly did not," Susan argued quietly. "I would never do that. Miss Brooks told me that you had told her it would be all right to come, Mr. Kincaid, that you were sure your uncle wouldn't mind."

Nellie snorted. "She's lying, Adam! Can't you see that?"

"Susan does not lie, I'll have you know!" Joshua said in her defense. "If anybody's lying, it's you, Nellie."

"Oh, this is just terrible," the older woman half sobbed. "I do so regret your having to be upset this way, and I must tell you it really hurts me to know you think I'm lying."

"Oh, for heaven's sake!" Adam interjected. "Enough of this nonsense. No matter how you got here, Nellie, it's obvious you brought too many people and you're disturbing Uncle Josh. You'd better just pack up and go."

"But we're not finished!"

"Yes, you are! You're not going to stay another minute in my Meredith's garden!"

When Joshua swayed slightly after issuing his command, Susan saw how unnaturally pale he looked, perspiration beading above his upper lip. She hurried to his side, taking his arm.

"I think I better get him upstairs," she told Adam. "He's very tired."

"Yes, yes, do that," he said, his concern obvious. "Do you need some help?"

"I'm not an invalid," Joshua answered for her. "But many more days like this and I may be."

Nellie sobbed again. "Oh, Mr. Thornton, I—"

"Come upstairs before you leave, Adam," Joshua interrupted her as he leaned heavily on Susan's arm. "I want to talk with you privately."

As she walked with him out the door, Susan glanced back over her shoulder and heaved a silent sigh as she saw Nellie plucking appealingly at the sleeve of Adam's gray pin-striped suit. No doubt she would have quite a story to tell him, and no doubt he would believe every word of it.

Although Joshua was not actually experiencing any pain, he was completely exhausted and it did not take too much encouragement to get him to stretch out on the bed.

"Don't you worry," he said reassuringly. "I'll make sure Adam knows exactly what went on here today. He'll see it was not your fault."

"I'm not worried," Susan lied cheerfully as she covered him with a green and gold afghan. "Now you try to go to sleep." Then she tiptoed out to let him get some rest.

It was a relief to go into her own room and shut the

door behind her. She too was tired and the high canopied bed looked very inviting. Kicking off her shoes, she stretched out across the yellow quilted bedspread, resting her head on her folded arms.

What kind of lies would Nellie tell Adam, she wondered almost indifferently, feeling it really did not matter what *she* told him. After all, he knew Nellie; she was his friend while Susan was practically a stranger. And that disastrous confrontation at the studio would have to influence him.

"Oh, you idiot," she muttered self-derisively. Why couldn't she have refrained that day from slipping back into her childhood? Calling him a big jerk had been a reaction she should have left in pre-adolescence, and she wished again that she could relive that day. If she could have a second chance, she would simply laugh at him for mistaking her for a would-be model, then walk away, leaving him to wonder forever what she found so amusing.

But hindsight did her no good right now when she had little hope that Adam's first impression of her would allow him to even give her the benefit of the doubt. Nellie might even be so convincing in her lies that he could decide she was such a horrid person that his uncle should know how they had first met. What would Joshua think of her then, she wondered as she lifted herself up off the bed and went to brush her windblown hair with such quick, brisk strokes that it crackled. As she smoothed the flyaway strands, someone knocked on the door. Realizing it might very well be Adam, she took a deep breath as she smoothed the skirt of her beige jersey dress, then opened the door unwillingly.

It was Adam.

"May I come in?" he asked quietly, his expression indefinable.

Her bedroom was the last place she wished to have a discussion with him, but she had no idea how to tell him that without proving herself to be the fool he thought she was. So she simply motioned him inside, but his closing the door behind him did nothing for her peace of mind.

Turning back to face him, she stood very still in the center of the room, clenching her hands together behind her, waiting as he leaned back against the closed door.

"I've just had a talk with Uncle Josh and he assures me that you were telling the truth downstairs," he said after a long, tense silence, "but, of course, Nellie insists that she was."

"Of course," Susan murmured.

"Is that all you have to say?"

She shrugged, chewing her lower lip unhappily. "Would it do me any good to say anything else?"

"Why don't you try it and find out?"

Her eyes darted up to his face, but his expression still told her nothing.

"All right, I was telling the truth, about all of it. Nellie was lying. Now, do you believe that?"

He said nothing, but, after a horrendously long moment when he simply looked at her, he stood up straight. And with two long strides he was close in front of her, lifting her chin with one finger, gazing deeply into her wide violet eyes as if he expected to find the truth in them.

"I don't know what to make of you," he whispered. "I know what you can be like, but I know what Nellie can be like too. She's never been above telling lies to get something done if that something can further her career. But you don't like her and I wonder if you could have engineered this entire situation so she would look bad. Could you have?"

Susan shook her head slowly. "No, I couldn't have done that. My mind doesn't work that deviously."

"Doesn't it? Wouldn't you call it devious that you

came to work for Uncle Josh hoping you could then persuade me to give you a modeling job?"

"I've told you I had no idea he was your uncle," she said, starting to take a step backward, then tensing as he reached out and gripped her shoulders. Before she thought, her hands came up to press lightly against his chest, feeling the warmth of his body even through the fabric of his vest and shirt. "I didn't know he was, really. I wish you'd believe me."

"I wish I could," he said softly, his dark gaze lingering for a disturbing moment on her mouth. "Uncle Josh is getting very attached to you, just as I was afraid he would. So I'd certainly rest easier at night if I knew you could be trusted."

"I can be," she replied, trying to ignore the sudden, nearly overwhelming need to have him kiss her as he had kissed her before. "You can trust me—I like your uncle very much and I'd never do anything to upset him."

"Good," Adam said, his tone suddenly brusque as he abruptly released her arms and walked to the door, not even looking back as he opened it and went out.

Chapter Five

The following Saturday a few of the models returned with Nellie—but this time Adam also came along, so the completion of the series of photographs was far different than the beginning had been. No one even knocked on the door of the house; a small trailer had been brought for the models to change in, and apparently any refreshment that was required was brought in from the outside, because Emily was not ordered to provide any.

As usual Susan and Joshua worked through the morning and without interruption were able to make good progress, so that by lunchtime Joshua was in a particularly jolly mood.

"So how are you going to spend your afternoon off today?" he asked Susan as they had their coffee after the meal. "Baker is available to drive you into town if you'd like to go shopping."

"No, I don't think so, thank you. I'd rather just explore around here if you wouldn't mind my taking Penny out again."

"Why should I mind? I wish I could go with you, though. I always enjoyed riding. That was one of the main reasons I never considered selling this old place. When Cathy was small, Meredith and I would take her with us when we went out, and it was amazing how unafraid she was even when we went galloping off across the fields."

As he stared off into space then, a reminiscent smile on his lips, Susan looked away. He seemed so lonely sometimes, even when she was talking to him, that she felt like crying. It was such a shame he had been left all alone with nothing but his memories. But at least he did not try to live excessively in the past. Even now, he was rousing himself from his pensive mood to smile endearingly at her.

"I thought maybe you'd forgo your ride today to go out and see what Adam and his crowd are up to."

It was the last thing Susan would ever have considered doing, but she refrained from saying so. "I wouldn't want to get in anybody's way," she said instead. "I know they must want to get finished as quickly as possible."

"Oh, I'm sure Adam wouldn't mind if you wanted to watch."

"I think I'd just as soon take Penny out."

Joshua frowned slightly. "You don't feel very comfortable around Adam, do you?" he asked. "I've noticed from the very beginning that you seem to get jumpy whenever he comes over here. What's the matter? Don't you like him?"

"He doesn't like me," she murmured without looking at him. She wished he hadn't brought up this subject, because she had no desire to lie to him. Yet she did not feel she could tell him about her first meeting with his nephew. And she was begrudgingly grateful to Adam for not telling his uncle himself, though she did not really understand why he hadn't. It seemed to her that he was the type of man who would enjoy embarrassing her, if only to pay her back for calling him names in front of the people he worked with. It was baffling, like a puzzle with some of the pieces missing, and, frankly, she was tired of trying to work it out. She attempted a nonchalant wave of her hand. "I suppose I'm just not the kind of girl that appeals to him."

"Now, why would you say that?"

"Oh, I guess I'm not pretty and sophisticated enough for Adam to bother with. You know, I just wouldn't ever fit into his world."

"I think that should be considered an attribute," Joshua responded surprisingly. "I love my nephew but I don't always approve of his lifestyle. Those people he considers his friends don't impress me much, especially the women. It's bad enough for a man to flit from one relationship to another, but a woman . . ." Shaking his head, he reached across the table to pat Susan's hand. "You're wrong, though, about not being pretty. You're a very lovely girl, and I'm sure Adam thinks so too."

"Has he said so? He probably would have if he thought I was."

"I'm not sure I understand that logic," Joshua said bewilderedly. "I've never been his confidant when it came to his feelings about young ladies. He's always made that a very personal part of his life, which I think is a wise decision. Romantic relationships can be complicated enough without involving outsiders."

"Do you think he'll ever marry?" Susan asked impulsively, blushing slightly as she realized how interested in Adam the question made her sound. "Never mind," she amended hastily. "I shouldn't have asked you that."

"Why not? It's a question I've asked myself many times in the past few years, but I'm afraid I still don't have an answer. He might marry if he could find a woman who suited him, but I'm not all that sure he really knows what he's looking for. So . . ."

"Many people don't really know what they want, I suppose."

"And are you one of them? Do you know what

you're looking for in a man? What would you want in a husband?"

"Oh, somebody considerate and honest and kind."

"A real Boy Scout, eh?" Joshua teased.

"Well, no, I didn't mean—"

"I know what you meant and I agree with you to some extent. You should find somebody considerate and honest, but there'll have to be more, you know. There has to be that certain magic you both feel when you're together. Marriage isn't ever easy, even when a man and a woman love each other very much. And if they don't, it's usually nearly impossible."

"Yes, probably so," Susan murmured as she shifted in her chair. Then she lifted questioning eyebrows as Joshua laughed lightly. "Did I say something funny?"

"No, not at all. It's just that I can see you're aching to get outside, but that's only natural since you're cooped up in here with me all day every day."

"But I get out an hour or so every evening before it gets dark," she reminded him. "So I don't feel cooped up, really."

"Nevertheless, you're eager to get out to Penny right now, so why don't you go on and change your clothes and do just that? I'm going upstairs to rest for a while anyway."

"You're sure you won't need me for anything?"

"I'm sure. Now, scoot," he insisted, waving her away.

Ten minutes later, after dressing in jeans and a red-and-black flannel shirt, Susan bounded down the wide veranda steps and headed around the side of the house. It was cooler now than it had been early in the day because the bright early-autumn sun had been blocked by gray clouds that seemed to be getting more ominously dark with each passing minute. She went on anyway, assured by Baker's promise that it would not actually start to rain before evening. Since he based his prediction on the severity of pain in his arthritic knee, she was convinced she could trust him. After all, he had not yet been wrong in his forecasts since her arrival at Maiden's Bower.

Besides, there was something invigorating about a cloudy autumn day. The cool, crisp breeze caressed her with the homey aroma of hickory smoke and she inhaled appreciatively as she walked across the backyard past the grape arbor to the tall evergreen hedge that separated the lawn and the extensive barnyard beyond. But as she opened the white gate in the center of the hedge she stopped short, sighing with dismay at the sight of the group of people gathered at the paddock. She had hoped Adam and his associates had finished here and left, but they were still photographing. Nellie Brooks was running around frantically, positioning five models so that the casual yet expensive clothing they wore would be shown to best advantage. And one of the models was Barbara, dressed in a classic tweed suit, her blond hair pulled back in a sleek chignon.

Susan smiled. Barbara had been so excited when she called Thursday night, saying she would be working here today. Wearing classy clothes for a magazine layout, she had quipped, certainly beat being a French fry. If only the layout could have been photographed elsewhere, Susan thought, chewing her fingernail nervously, hoping Barbara wouldn't decide to tell someone the two of them were related. She could be making a serious mistake if she did. Her modeling career could be jeopardized if Adam or Nellie learned she and Susan were cousins, and Susan had warned her of such a possibility Thursday night. Unfortunately, Barbara was feeling much more secure lately and she hadn't taken the warning very seriously.

Fearing her cousin might decide to risk acknowledging her, Susan sighed worriedly, twisting a strand of hair around her finger. Maybe she should just go back to the house instead of taking Penny out. Yet she was reluctant to forgo the ride she had been looking forward to all morning. Surely if she walked past the group while the photographers were actually taking pictures, Barbara would have no chance to acknowledge her.

She was going, she decided, lifting her chin resolutely. As she passed the paddock she glanced up only once, but it was not to look Barbara's way. Instead, her eyes were drawn to Adam, who stood apart from the others, his hands thrust into the pockets of his corduroy trousers, watching her approach. As he inclined his head slightly in greeting, she forced a tight little smile in response, not allowing herself to quicken her pace to get past him.

Once inside the sturdy red barn, however, she did feel much more at ease and she hurried to Penny's stall, eager to get her saddled and be off. The mare seemed glad to see her and nuzzled her shoulder gently.

"You'll get your sugar; just be patient," Susan said, laughing as the horse sniffed at the pocket of her flannel shirt. "Let me get you out of there first."

"Aren't you afraid sugar might be bad for her?" Adam suddenly asked from the open barn door.

Shaking her head, trying to ignore the rapid beating of her heart, Susan watched as he came into the barn toward her.

"I only give her a sugar cube right before I take her out," she murmured in explanation. "Since that's only two or three times a week, I don't think it'll do her any harm. Do you?" Then, without waiting for an answer, she turned back to unlatch the stall door, wishing he had just stayed outside, instead of coming in here to harass her. Sensing he was watching her closely, she slipped the bridle over Penny's head with slightly shaking hands, then led her out into barn, positioning her so that she was between Adam and herself, but to no avail.

Patting Penny gently, he came around to Susan's side just as she dug into her shirt pocket for the cube of sugar. After she had pulled it out only to let it slip through her fingers, he picked it up off the dirt floor and handed it back.

"Thank you," she whispered, willing herself not to jerk her hand away when his hard fingertips brushed across the sensitive skin of her palm. Hating herself for the warmth that suddenly rushed to her cheeks, she half turned away to hold the sugar in her cupped hand beneath Penny's nose. "There you go, girl."

"How easy is she for you to handle?" he asked abruptly as she hoisted the saddle onto the horse's back, then cinched the girth. "She was pretty skittish when I bought her about six months ago, but I hoped she'd settle down."

"You mean she's yours?" Susan exclaimed softly, her heart sinking when he nodded. "Oh, I didn't realize. Your uncle didn't mention that she belonged to you when I asked if he minded if I rode her. I'm sorry."

As she started to uncinch the saddle, Adam's large hand shot out to still her own. "Why are you doing that?" he asked, frowning. "I thought you were going to take her out for a while."

Susan eased her hand out from beneath his to stroke Penny's gleaming copper mane. "I didn't know she belonged to you."

"And it makes a difference that she does?"

Unable to look at him, she nodded. "I'm sure you're not all that pleased that I've been riding her."

"You're wrong," he declared surprisingly and with some impatience. "I appreciate your riding her when you can. She needs more exercise than the boy I hired can give her. So, actually, you're doing me a favor."

"You're sure you mean that?" Susan questioned hopefully, her eyes brightening. "I mean, if you'd rather I not ride her, I—"

"What do you want? Permission in writing?" he

asked, a hint of a smile tugging at the corners of his mouth. "I just said I didn't mind, didn't I? Just finish saddling her and go . . . unless you'd really prefer to stay here and watch the photography session instead. You might be interested in seeing how much work goes into it. You could even change your mind about going into modeling after you see it's not as glamorous an occupation as most people imagine."

It was the trace of mockery in his tone that finally brought an end to Susan's patience. As she looked up at him, her violet eyes took on an icy glitter and indignation loosened her tongue. "All right. That does it! I've had all of this I can stand," she said heatedly. "You've been completely wrong about me from the beginning, Mr. Kincaid, you and that nitwit, Nellie. If the two of you had let me open my mouth before shoving me out of the studio that day, I could have told you then that I was only there because my cousin was in that commercial. It was her portfolio I had. Not everybody wants to be a model, Mr. Kincaid. *I* came to Atlanta looking for a job on a newspaper but I wasn't having any luck at finding one. And, by the way, I met your uncle purely by chance. I certainly didn't approach him because I saw you talking to him in the park. If I'd seen you with him I probably would have avoided him like the plague—the last thing I ever wanted was to see you again, after the way you'd treated me."

Pausing to take a breath, Susan smirked at the look of pure astonishment on Adam's tanned face. "So there. Now that you finally realize you were wrong about me, you can stop telling me I'm not attractive enough to be a model. I'm tired of hearing you say I'm a physical disaster."

Thrusting her chin up, she led Penny past Adam, through the open doors and out onto the hard-packed red clay. Her heart pounding with delayed reaction, she mounted the horse hastily, eager to get far away from there. As usual she had let that impossible man upset her, and she wondered bleakly why she could not just once manage to remain cool and unruffled in his presence.

"Oh, just forget about him," she told herself impatiently.

Pushing all disturbing thoughts aside, she guided Penny along the narrow tractor trace that led past the peach orchard to the fields. But after they passed over a small incline and she knew they could no longer be seen from the barn, she urged the horse into an easy, graceful canter across a freshly tilled field. The brisk wind lifted her hair up off her shoulders, chilling her cheeks and bringing a sparkle of exhilaration to her eyes. Before her stood a grove of maple trees, their remaining leaves brilliant orange even beneath an overcast sky, and Susan was eager to reach it, knowing that a secluded path led through it along the riverbank.

"Not so fast, girl," she said softly, slowing Penny to a trot as they entered the grove. But controlling her was more difficult now and Susan knew why. Beyond the trees was a rolling pasture where she always stopped to let Penny graze while she sat atop a large boulder and watched the river below flow past.

When a glimpse of browning green appeared between the tree trunks a few minutes later, Penny suddenly broke into a canter that nearly became a gallop, and Susan merely leaned forward in the saddle, letting her go as she pleased since it would have taken a great deal of pulling on the reins to curb her. Besides, she stopped quickly enough as soon as they reached the succulent grass she wanted to munch.

Susan dismounted and wrapped the reins around the lower branches of a small pine tree, leaving enough slack for the horse to widen her field of grazing. Then, sighing contentedly, she walked to the edge of the riverbank, kicking aside the dying vegetation that tried to entwine itself around her brown leather boots. The water level was somewhat lower than it had been last Saturday and the tops of several worn-smooth rocks created a small patch of rapids directly below where she stood. The soft, rushing sound the water made as it cascaded over the stones was somehow soothing, almost mesmerizing Susan so that she did not even notice the thudding of approaching hoofbeats on the hard-packed path beneath the trees until they suddenly ceased. Then the silence permeated her consciousness.

Startled that she was obviously no longer alone, she spun around in time to watch Adam dismount in one fluid movement from the beautiful bay stallion that occupied the stall across from Penny's.

"Oh, glory, what now?" she asked herself aloud. He looped the bay's reins around the branches of the same tree to which she had tethered Penny. Susan's heart began beating furiously, the rate of its pounding not decreasing in the least as he turned, then stood motionless, looking at her.

Even as she groaned softly, she forced a puzzled smile and was astonished when she received an almost sheepish one in return. She had not expected such a response and could not help staring at him rather foolishly as he strode down the hill toward her, the muscles of his long legs straining against the corduroy fabric of his trousers.

He said nothing as he stopped beside her. Reaching inside his navy-blue crewneck sweater, he pulled a pack of cigarettes from his shirt pocket and held it out to her.

She took one. Not that she was a regular smoker—she wasn't—but right now she wanted something to do with her hands. Yet, when he held out his lighter and she instinctively touched her fingers to the back of his hand as he brought the flame against the end of her cigarette, she wished she had never accepted it. He had to have noticed the shakiness of her fingers against his skin. Chewing her upper lip, she looked away nervously as he lit his own. She sighed, and, when she did,

Adam gripped her arm gently and turned her around to face him.

"It seems I owe you an apology," he said softly, his green eyes dark as they swept over her face. "I guess you had every right to call me a big jerk."

A soft gasp escaped her as she stared up at him. She must be dreaming; that was the only explanation she could find. He had not really apologized—it had been a hallucination.

But it had not been. He smiled indulgently at her astonished expression and added, "One question, though. Why didn't you tell me the truth long before now?"

"I was afraid my cousin's career might suffer if you knew she was related to me," Susan answered candidly. "Actually, she's one of the models here today, but I can't tell you which one unless you promise—"

"You really think I'd treat her unfairly because she's your cousin?" Adam asked, something like dismay in his deep voice. "You must know I wouldn't do that, especially now, knowing how wrong I've been about you."

Susan grimaced. "I *did* call you a big jerk."

"And you had every right to, as I just said." Adam smiled down at her apologetically. "Nellie and I shouldn't have jumped to conclusions, and I'm terribly sorry we did."

Susan was absolutely speechless for a moment. A genuine apology from Adam Kincaid was the last thing she had ever imagined receiving. And it *was* genuine; something in the tone of his voice told her that. At last she managed to gesture weakly.

"It really wasn't all your fault," she found herself saying. "I-I'd already had a bad morning, and then Miss Brooks was not really very friendly when she told me to leave."

"Oh, I see. Nellie gave me the impression that you had simply refused to listen; that's why I tried to explain the situation to you. Or at least I thought I would. Obviously, I had no idea what I was talking about."

Susan smiled wanly. "Oh, well, it doesn't really matter now, I guess."

"But I think it does," he disagreed, his hands on her arm tightening as he drew her slightly closer. "Our behavior was very rude, and I can't blame you for being upset by it."

"I was pretty rude myself," she admitted with a self-conscious little smile. "I never should have called you what I did."

"I've been called worse," he replied with a wry, endearing grin. "But I must say you managed to convey a great deal of contempt in those two simple little words."

"I didn't mean to say them so loudly. I never dreamed all those people were watching and listening. Blurting that out embarrassed me as much as you, I think."

"Yes, I know it did," he said gently.

"Why don't we just forget about it—forget it ever happened?" she murmured nervously when he did not release her. "I accept your apology."

"But I haven't finished making it. I said some very unpleasant things to you that night I drove you home, and my actions were even worse. I'm truly sorry. It was very arrogant of me to believe you had approached Uncle Josh in the park simply because you had seen me talking to him. My only excuse is that girls often dream up elaborate schemes to try to get themselves modeling jobs, and of course I assumed you were one of them."

"I'm not," she answered, attempting an unconcerned smile. But that was no easy accomplishment since Adam's fingers around her arm had loosened their grip and begun a light stroking motion that was sending shivers of awareness throughout her body. She swallowed with difficulty, lowering her eyes to the strong column of his brown neck extending from the open collar of his shirt. "I-I don't want to be a model. I've never wanted to be one. Which is just as well, isn't it, since I'm not nearly attractive enough?"

"Susan," he whispered chidingly, his hand sliding up over her shoulder to cup her neck beneath the thickness of her hair. "If you're trying to imply that I told you you're not attractive, then you're wasting your time. I know I never would have said that, because it simply isn't true."

The caressing way he had said her name had set her pulses racing, and now the mysterious light in his eyes was making the excitement almost unbearable. "But you did say I was too short," she argued weakly. "And not nearly sophisticated enough."

"Yes, I did, but I meant that only in regard to modeling. You would have had a difficult time getting jobs because you're not quite tall enough and because you look younger than you actually are. But that certainly doesn't mean you're not beautiful. In fact, innocence in a woman's face may be the most beautifying quality she can possess. And you have that, Susan," he murmured softly. "And the most exquisite eyes I've ever seen."

"Do I?" she whispered breathlessly, her legs weakening beneath her as he pulled her closer, closer, until she felt the warm hardness of his thighs pressing against her. Gazing up at him, she moistened her dry lips with the tip of her tongue, and unintentionally provocative action that brought an immediate and passionate reaction.

"Susan!" He groaned, sliding his arms around her waist, crushing her soft young body against the hardness of his as his mouth sought her own.

Even that night in his car, he had not kissed her the way he was kissing her now, and Susan surrendered eagerly to the bruising power of his arms and seeking lips that were parting hers with irresistible demand.

When he suddenly swept her up into his arms, she wrapped her own around his neck as he carried her up the hill, then laid her down gently on the soft grass. Kneeling beside her, his dark gaze holding hers, he reached down to trace one fingertip across the parted fullness of her lips until she moaned softly.

"Kiss me!" he demanded huskily as the lean length of his body pressed her down into the grass and he took her mouth again with a savage hunger that seemed beyond the control of either of them.

Certainly it was beyond Susan's control. She trembled violently as he turned over onto his side, pulling her with him. And she found it impossible to protest even when he unbuttoned her shirt with unsteady fingers, then spread his hand possessively over the bare sensitive skin of her stomach.

"I *want* you!" he muttered roughly, pushing aside the straps of her brief bra, seeking the generous curve of her breast above it with warm, firm lips.

Aroused more than she had ever imagined she could be, Susan could only knead the corded muscles of his broad back, gasping softly as his hands on her hips pressed her close against him.

"You imagined I didn't think you're beautiful," he whispered as his teeth closed gently on the sweet fullness of her lower lip. "What a child you are! But what a beautiful, desirable child, and I can't seem to keep my hands off you."

"Adam!" she whispered back urgently, twining her fingers in the silvery thickness of his hair, seeking his mouth with her own.

But after a few more intense minutes he pulled away abruptly, dragging her slender arms from around his neck. With a groan, he turned over onto his back, draping his arm across his closed eyes.

"I must be insane, getting myself involved with you," he muttered. "I thought I had more sense."

A sudden burning ache gathered quickly behind

Susan's eyes. Biting down hard on her lip, she turned her head to one side, staring blindly toward the trees. What a fool she was, she thought, her entire body heating with humiliation. All the time she had been delighting in his touch, he had been hating himself for touching her. But why? He had said he thought she was beautiful, and now that he knew she was not the silly character he had believed her to be, why should he feel ashamed? It didn't make any sense. One large tear escaped from beneath her closed lid, then she stiffened as Adam's hand covered hers.

"I didn't mean that the way it sounded," he said gently, sitting up, then pulling her up beside him. Cupping her face in his large hands, he brushed the tear away with his thumb. "Listen—you're just too young for me and so inexperienced. I can't allow myself to take advantage of you."

"I'm not a child," she muttered defensively, her eyes glittering with hurt and a little anger. "I can take care of myself. *I* won't allow you to take advantage of me."

"Oh, Susan, I don't think you realize how easily feelings like these can go beyond anybody's control." His eyes darkened momentarily as he gazed at the parted softness of her lips, but then he shook his head. "Don't you see? We're attracted to each other—we have been since the very first day. Lord knows I don't want to follow in old Jonathan Thornton's footsteps and seduce you the way he did Felicity." When Susan blushed, his thumbs on her cheeks became caressing and he smiled indulgently. "They met here every day for weeks, right here by the river where we are. Did you know that?"

She shook her head, her eyes confused and very unhappy. "But what's that got to do with—"

"This is where it happened, so the story goes." Adam shrugged, massaging the back of his neck with one hand. "I can understand it, can't you? It's very secluded here, and they had been attracted to each other for several months. He wanted her, Susan, and she was too young to know how to handle that kind of desire. And it's obvious to me that you're too young to know how to handle it, either."

"I'm not seventeen!" she protested vehemently. "I'll be twenty-two soon."

"But you're no more experienced in these matters than she was!"

"You're not the first man who's ever kissed me! I haven't been hiding in a closet all my life. I've actually been out alone with men."

"Men my age?" he asked calmly. "Or young men your age?"

As Susan looked down at her clenched hands, unwilling to answer, she realized with some embarrassment that her shirt was still unbuttoned. She hastily clutched the lapels together and her eyes darted back up to his face when he chuckled knowingly.

"You see what I mean? You know you're playing with fire, don't you? You know I won't be satisfied with a few frantic kisses in the car, the way the *boys* you've been out with always were."

"All right, all right, yes, I know that! I know you're used to women with much more experience than I have." She gestured helplessly. "I just forgot, I guess, that you'd expect—"

"But I don't expect anything. I never did," he said softly, his eyes sweeping over her. "I know you'd never be happy with that kind of relationship, and I don't intend to let anything happen that might hurt you the way Felicity must have been hurt."

For a moment she almost believed he was genuinely concerned about her happiness, but suddenly she recalled what he had said that night in his car. "You needn't pretend you're worried about what might happen to me," she said stiffly. "I know that's not what's really bothering you. I remember what you said about not getting involved with an inexperienced girl because she might decide she wanted to marry you. That's really what you're saying, isn't it? That you don't want to take the chance of being trapped into marriage the way Jonathan was?" She scrambled to her feet and stood glaring down at him. "Well, you don't have to worry about that happening with me, because it won't. Even if I were foolish enough to get involved with you that way, which I'm not, I'd never expect you to marry me. This is not 1840, and I'm not Felicity. I'd rather take care of myself any old day than force a man to marry me when he didn't want to."

When she spun around then and started marching away, he jumped up, catching her wrist in a painful grip.

"Susan, I didn't mean—"

"I know exactly what you meant," she muttered, staring at the hand that held her arm. "I may not be sophisticated, but that doesn't mean I'm stupid." Jerking her wrist free from his grasp, she half ran to untie Penny, propelled herself up onto the saddle, then dug her heels into the mare's flanks.

As she urged Penny to take the path through the trees at a dangerous gallop, she did not look back once toward the pasture. When they finally came out of the grove into the adjoining field and began to speed across it, she wondered disgustedly why people like Adam thought being sophisticated meant they had to be incapable of any deep emotion. And, more important, why did the fact that he thought that way disturb her much more than it should?

Chapter Six

For the next few days, Susan did her utmost to suppress all thoughts of Adam Kincaid. He was not worth worrying about anyway, she told herself. She had never liked shallow people, never even liked to be around them, so from now on until her work at Maiden's Bower was finished she would avoid him completely. And if she was forced to endure his company occasionally, she would not let him disturb her. If he had a thousand casual affairs, what did she care? If sleeping with anybody who came along made a person sophisticated, then she was glad she was not.

Maybe she was naïve, she considered frequently. Or maybe life in a small town like the one where she had grown up was just more old-fashioned and had instilled in her most of the old values that Adam and his crowd would consider hopelessly outdated. Or maybe she was just a dreamer, waiting around for that special man her mother had assured her she would find someday, that man who would be pleased she was inexperienced. But if she was a naïve, old-fashioned dreamer, it couldn't be helped. It had taken her nearly twenty-two years to become the young woman she now was, and she could probably never really change even if she wanted to. And she didn't want to. She would rather spend the rest of her life waiting for that special relationship than settle for something less with every man who came along. It all seemed like a frantic hopeless search to her—and terribly sad.

Yet, sure as she was that she and Adam wanted completely different kinds of lives, she knew he had been right when he said they were attracted to each other, at least physically, and she regretted that as much as he obviously did. Though she had been kissed many times before by young men older than she was and more handsome than Adam, not one of them had ever made her feel as alive as he had Saturday afternoon. And it seemed a shame that such an intensely exciting compatibility was going to be wasted, but unfortunately that was the way it had to be.

Joshua helped to keep her thoughts from wandering too often to his nephew. As their work on his family history progressed, his health almost seemed to improve. He slept less and sometimes wanted to work longer than Susan thought he should, but she couldn't bring herself to really discourage him. He seemed to be having such a good time, even after he caught a cold that developed into a bad cough. He felt fine, though, or so he insisted whenever she or Baker or Emily suggested he should see his doctor. But perhaps she should have done something to make him rest until his cold was better.

Susan felt as if she had only been asleep a few minutes when Emily came in to shake her awake about one o'clock Wednesday morning and it took a great effort on her part to simply open her eyes.

"What's the matter?" she muttered sleepily, trying to turn over and escape the woman's hands as they shook her shoulders. "Did I oversleep?"

"It's Mr. Joshua, Miss Thomas," Emily said, her voice shaky. "He's having an awful time breathing but he won't let us call the doctor for him. I thought maybe you could talk to him. You know how he is—he won't listen to a thing we say."

Wide awake now, Susan sat up in bed, shivering in

her cotton nightgown. "What do you mean, he's having trouble breathing?" she asked worriedly. "Do you think it's just his cold or . . . or do you think it could be something worse?"

"Lord, I don't know," Emily answered as she stood by the bed, twisting her hands together in front of her. "All I know's he's laying in there, gasping for breath."

Susan got up, picked up her robe off the chair by the bed, and thrust her arms into it. "Is he in any pain?" she asked the housekeeper.

"He's says no, but he looks real bad to me."

"Then go ahead and call the doctor—I'll take the blame if he gets mad," Susan told her as she hurried toward the door. "Call him now while I go talk to him."

Joshua's room was three doors down from her own, and when she went in Baker was hovering beside the huge four-poster bed, twisting his hands just as his wife had done. "Talk to him, miss," he pleaded almost pitifully. "He needs to have a doctor, but he won't listen to a word I say to him."

"Oh, stop exaggerating, Baker; you're scaring the girl for nothing," Joshua managed to scold between fits of coughing. He smiled weakly up at Susan. "It's nothing to worry about, really, so go on back to bed. You need your rest."

"And you need a doctor," she answered, frowning when he winced slightly as he coughed again. "You're in pain, aren't you? Where does it hurt?"

He laid a limp hand in the general area of his breastbone. "Oh, it just hurts a little here when I cough."

When he reached out that hand toward her, Susan took it and sat down on the edge of the bed. "I told Emily to go ahead and call the doctor for you," she informed him without apology, shaking her head when he started to protest. "Now, you know he needs to check you over. You've let this cold go on too long."

He shook his head in mock admonition. "What's

this? Don't tell me you're going to start helping Baker nag me."

Susan did not smile. "If I have to nag, it's only because you're being so stubborn. If you're sick, why are you so reluctant to have the doctor come? There's no use feeling bad when he might be able to give you something to make you better."

"And he might tell me to stop working on the Thornton history," Joshua replied, his expression solemn now. "Did you ever think of that?"

"But I don't think he'd tell you to give it up completely," she argued gently. "He just might want you to slow down a little, which would probably be a very good idea. You've been doing too much the past several days."

His hand tightened around hers. "But when you're my age, you have to get things done quickly or you might never get a chance to do them at all."

"But what good does it do to go quickly if it ends up making you sick? Then you can't do anything at all for a while, can you?" Susan said, patting his shoulder as she stood. "Now, you just lie there while I go ask Emily what the doctor said."

"No, let Baker go," Joshua whispered raspingly. "If I have to have my hand held, then I'd rather you held it."

As she sat down again, Susan grinned at the man still hovering by the bed. "He isn't all that sick, is he, Baker?" she said reassuringly. "He's still flirting." When he nodded and forced a wan little smile, she added: "Why don't you go see what the doctor said, all right?"

But he hardly had a chance to move before his wife leaned around the doorjamb. "The doctor said he'd be here as soon as he could, miss," she whispered loudly. "It shouldn't be long—he lives just down the road."

The next ten minutes dragged by as Susan sat on the edge of the bed, watching Joshua drift off to sleep between spates of coughing. He did look very pale, and she didn't like the heavy wheezing sound she heard with every breath he took. It was a great relief when she finally heard heavy footsteps in the hall and then Emily ushered Dr. Jennings into the room.

Susan had met the doctor before when he dropped by one afternoon for a chat with Joshua and she liked him. David Jennings was a tall, heavyset man who smiled often and made jokes, but tonight he was not smiling. He nodded a greeting in her direction as she moved out of his way; then he took a stethoscope from his bag and leaned over the bed to listen to Joshua's breathing.

"Well, now, that doesn't sound very good," he commented after a moment. He straightened, shaking his head as Joshua opened his eyes. "Trying to make trouble for me, aren't you?" he chided, though not unkindly. "You've got a nice case of bronchitis there that needs clearing up before it turns into pneumonia and then you really are in a mess." He turned to Baker. "Why don't you pack him a few things, then we'll take him on in to the hospital?"

"Hospital! I don't need to go to the hospital! Why can't you just give me something and let me stay here?"

"And why don't you let me be the doctor here?" David Jennings retorted. "I'd feel much better if you were admitted. Now, are you going to cooperate, or do Baker and I have to carry you down to my car?"

"Don't have much choice, do I?" Joshua mumbled grumpily. "But there's no need to drag Baker along with us. He's nearly as feeble as I am."

"That ain't so, Mr. Joshua!" Baker protested vehemently, glaring back over his shoulder as he took a pair of pajamas from a dresser drawer. "And I'm going with you to the hospital; you ain't going there all by yourself."

Joshua grimaced. "Don't let him go, Dave," he said firmly. "He's got a bad cold too. Going out in this cold night air will just make him worse—and, besides, you don't want him spreading germs all over the hospital."

"Maybe you just better stay here, then, Baker," Dr. Jennings suggested as he closed his black bag. "I can get him there all right without help."

Baker turned around, his lips pressed together in a reproachful pout. "But he ought not have to go by himself."

"Then Susan will go with me," Joshua said, obviously seeing that Baker was extremely upset. "Won't you, Susan?"

"Oh, yes, of course," she said hastily. "Just give me time to throw on some clothes."

After Susan threw on a blouse and skirt and gave her tousled hair a haphazard brushing, she helped Baker and Dr. Jennings get Joshua down to the car, where he lay down on the back seat. Then they sped away to the brightly lighted hospital on the outskirts of Atlanta.

It was only after an orderly pushed Joshua's wheelchair down the wide corridor that Dr. Jennings really expressed his concern.

"I think Josh's nephew should be called right away. Do you know Adam?" he asked and, when she nodded, he continued, "Would you give him a call while I go see that Josh gets started on the antibiotic?"

After she had agreed and he had walked away, she went looking for a telephone.

"I'll be right there," Adam said even before she could finish explaining.

And twenty minutes later he came rushing into the waiting room, raking his fingers through his thick hair as he approached her.

Pushing aside all thoughts of their last encounter, Susan answered his questions concerning his uncle's condition as best she could.

With a weary sigh, Adam sank down on the sofa beside her. "Did Dr. Jennings say how long he'd be?" he asked after a moment. "I'd like to talk to him."

"I'm sure he'll be back soon. He just wanted to be sure the medication was started immediately."

"What made Uncle Josh let his cold get this bad?" he whispered urgently. "He's not usually so stubborn that he won't see a doctor when he needs one."

"He said he was afraid Dr. Jennings would tell him to stop working on his family history," Susan said rather guiltily. "So I wonder if this is partly my fault. If I hadn't agreed to help him write it, he probably wouldn't have gotten involved in it at all and he wouldn't be in here right now."

"But you can't blame yourself for this, Susan," Adam said, taking her hand in his. "It's certainly not your fault that he wouldn't take proper care of himself."

"But I feel that it is."

"Well, I know you're wrong. If anything, you've done Uncle Josh a lot of good in the past few weeks. It's been a long time since I've seen him act so excited about anything."

"Really?" she asked, her violet eyes searching his face as if she could not actually believe him. But she saw no sign of dishonesty in the warm depths of the green eyes that were meeting hers. "I'm glad he's enjoyed doing it. But I don't want to see him get really sick because of it."

"I think he'd rather do that than just sit out there in that big house for the rest of his life with nothing to do," Adam told her. "He was always such an active man, and I think working on this history with you has done him more good than harm."

She smiled gratefully, then looked away. The silence that followed was not uncomfortable, which surprised her. After what had happened between them on Saturday, she would not ever have imagined they could be alone together again without feeling greatly ill at ease. But perhaps she should have known better. After all, Adam was an intelligent man. He would not let their differences of opinion take precedence over their mutual concern for his uncle. At least in that they could be in agreement.

It was nearly an hour later, about three thirty, when Dr. Jennings came walking into the waiting room. Adam stood to talk to him while Susan perched herself forward on the edge of the sofa.

"He's resting comfortably at the moment," was the doctor's first comment.

"Come on, Dave, don't give us that old standard hospital dodge," Adam said wryly. "Exactly how is he?"

"All right, he's a pretty sick man. You know breathing problems aren't doing a thing for his weak heart. I've started him on oxygen and antibiotics."

"Could we see him?" Adam asked, then reached down for Susan's hand. "Both of us?"

"Just for a minute or two. And don't get upset if he doesn't really recognize you. His fever's pretty high right now and sometimes he's delirious. He was calling for Meredith right before I left."

Yet, when Adam and Susan went into the small, dimly lighted room on the second floor a few minutes later, Joshua seemed to be sleeping quite peacefully.

"Are you Mr. Thornton's son?" she asked in a whisper.

Adam shook his head. "Nephew."

"Oh, I see. Well, unless you're just anxious to stay here, I think you and your wife would be doing yourselves a favor by going home."

"Oh, but we're not . . ." Susan began.

"Now, I know you hate to go and leave him," the nurse interrupted. "But there's really nothing you can do if you stay here except wear yourselves out."

A mischievous gleam lit Adam's eyes as he smiled down at Susan.

"Let's just go and let him rest," Adam said softly and Susan started to step away from the bed. But before she could move, Joshua's eyes opened and he reached out toward her.

"Cathy," he whispered hoarsely. "Go on home and rest now. Just try to come back early in the morning, okay?"

Susan's startled eyes darted to Adam's face, but he only indicated with a nod that she should humor his uncle.

She leaned over the bed railing to lightly kiss Joshua's cheek. "I'll be here so early you won't even be awake yet, I promise."

"I always knew you were the best daughter in the world," he murmured.

When a soft sob escaped Susan, Adam took her arm to lead her out into the hall, then handed her his handkerchief as they took the elevator downstairs. But the hard knot of unshed tears that constricted her throat made even thank you impossible to utter until they were inside his Porsche, driving away.

"He thought I was Catherine," she finally managed to say, her voice strained. "Oh, Adam, isn't it awful that she can't really be here? I feel so sorry for him. I know he thinks about her and Meredith so often."

"You look a lot like Cathy," he said abruptly, turning his head to look at her. "Has he ever told you that?"

"No! He's never mentioned it. I had no idea."

"He mentioned it to me right away," Adam continued. "Of course, I'd already noticed."

"That explains, then, why he's been so very kind to me," she said musingly. "I mean, he seemed really fond of me even that day in the park."

"Maybe that has something to do with it. But don't get the idea that he always thinks you *are* her. He knows you're not. I just think it pleases him to have a young lady in the house again, especially one with dark hair and lovely light eyes, though yours are violet and Cathy's were blue."

As Susan dried her tears with one corner of his handkerchief, she eyed him thoughtfully. "So *that's* why you wanted to be sure I wouldn't take this job, then just run out on him in a couple of weeks?" she said. "Isn't it?"

As he turned the car down a broad residential street, he nodded. "I thought it would be best that he didn't get accustomed to having you around if there was a chance you wouldn't stay with him long."

"I promised him I'd help him with this history, Adam," she reminded him softly. "I wouldn't walk out on him until it's done, not after promising."

He gave her a quick glance that almost seemed to convey confusion. "You mean you wouldn't quit on him if somebody offered you a job as a reporter, say next week? You'd stay with him even if the job was just what you'd been wanting?"

"Yes, I'd stay."

"You know," he said bemusedly, shaking his head, "I think I believe you."

Turning to look out the window at the fine old homes visible beneath the streetlights, Susan had some difficulty suppressing a smug little smile. It gave her extreme satisfaction to hear him admit he might have been wrong about her. But after a few more minutes passed, that satisfaction changed to puzzlement.

"Where are we going?" she asked as she realized they were driving through a section of town she had never traveled before. "Isn't this sort of an out-of-the-way route to Maiden's Bower."

"But we're not going to Maiden's Bower," Adam informed her. "If you want to be back at the hospital early, I see no sense in going all the way out there. Since it's nearly four o'clock, I decided we'd be better off just spending the night at my house."

"But I . . . you . . . I mean, that makes sense, b-but

we can't just spend the night together," she stammered. "Can we?"

"I don't see why not," he answered, amusement evident in his deep voice. "What's the matter? Don't you trust me? Will it help any to know my housekeeper will be right there to protect you?"

Susan heaved a sigh of relief. "Well, why didn't you say so in the first place?"

"Because it really shouldn't matter whether she's there or not. I told you Saturday that I have no intentions of starting an intimate relationship with you. Don't you remember?"

"I remember very clearly," she muttered. But she also remembered the passion that had flared between them, and she remembered that the kisses and caresses they had shared had made an intimate relationship seem infinitely desirable. But she supposed that since he had decided he wanted no more to do with her she would be safe spending the night in his house, especially with his housekeeper there to chaperon.

Besides, she wanted to see where he lived anyway, to see if the image her imagination had provided for her had been in any way correct. It had been, she discovered a few minutes later as Adam turned into a tree-lined driveway. His house sat in a stand of hardwood trees and, though its design was contemporary, its stained cedar exterior blended with the scenery and made it seem even more beautiful.

Hoping the interior was as charming, she got out of the car quickly when he opened her door, and they walked up the flagstone path to the massive front door. When they went inside, she was not disappointed. A spacious foyer opened onto a sunken living room with high cathedral ceilings with exposed beams. In the center of the room a huge round fireplace had been built of brick. Rust-colored velvet covered the two sofas and two chairs that sat on cream plush area rugs, and the entire room looked warm and welcoming.

"Oh, I love it!" she declared with unabashed enthusiasm, preceding him down the two steps into the room. "It's just beautiful!"

"I'm glad you like it." He gestured toward the sofa. "Would you like to sit down in here for a while, or would you rather go straight to bed?"

The deep, lazy cadence of his voice saying those words shocked her for some reason and she hated herself for the blush she felt creeping into her cheeks, especially when he noticed it and smiled indulgently.

"Maybe we better sit in here for a few minutes, until you get used to being here," he suggested. When she settled herself stiffly on the sofa, he sighed. "I didn't know you were going to be this nervous. I bet you'll never get to sleep. How about a drink? Maybe that would help."

"That would be nice," she murmured inadequately, wishing that just once she could maintain her composure around him. Now she was so embarrassed she could not even look at him as he went to the bar across the room. And she could only nod when he said he would have to get some ice.

After he left the room, she sighed and snuggled her cheek against the velvet sofa cushion, closing her eyes to the dim light. The next thing she knew she was being lifted up in Adam's strong arms and carried through the foyer down a long, wide hall. Too sleepy to protest, she merely draped her arms around his neck and burrowed her head deeper into the hollow of his shoulder, enjoying the feel of his brown crewneck sweater against her soft cheek.

"It's cold in here," she heard him mutter to himself, but she did not feel cold. His arms around her were delightfully warm, but when he jerked back the covers of the bed and then laid her down gently on the cool sheets she protested softly, tightening her arms around his neck.

"Umm, you're so warm," she murmured, smiling

lazily. And she was so relaxed in her drowsiness that she was completely unaware of how provocative her words and actions were. But obviously Adam was aware, because his darkening eyes held her gaze, alerting her even in her lethargy to the danger she was inviting.

"Adam," she whispered breathlessly, "I . . ."

"You're crazy, you know that, don't you?" he muttered roughly, slipping his arms completely around her slim waist, lifting her so that she lay across his thighs as he sat down on the bed.

Unable to resist his strength, Susan cupped his face in both her hands, exploring the contours of his ears with caressing fingertips.

"Kiss me," she found herself murmuring urgently as her gaze lingered on the sensual curve of his mouth. "Please kiss me."

"I need to do much more than that," he warned huskily even as he lowered his head to part her lips with the swift, demanding pressure of his.

Susan could only cling weakly to his shoulders as the hard hands that spanned her waist moved up to cover the straining fullness of her breasts. Suddenly they were lying on the bed as Adam's mouth took hers hungrily, as if he had waited too long for this moment. His strong fingers closed compellingly around her upper thigh, and even through the gabardine fabric of her skirt the intimate pressure of the heel of his hand ignited a burning ache throughout her body. She needed to be closer to him, much closer. But when she entwined her fingers in his hair, urging a rougher taking of her lips, Adam's hand slid beneath her skirt to brush upward along her thigh. A tremor shook her body, a tremor more of anticipation than of fear, but his hand was immediately still as he reluctantly dragged his mouth from hers.

"I didn't mean you could trust me this much," he muttered, his breathing uneven as he forced her arms from around his neck. "You're making it hard for me to remember you're a virgin."

An appealing blush crept into Susan's cheeks as her eyes met his for a brief, intense moment before he looked away and rose to his feet.

"I'll turn up the heat so you won't get cold," he said, his voice strained as he turned to walk to the door, where he adjusted the thermostat on the wall. Then, without even a backward glance, he went out, closing the door firmly behind him.

The sunlight streaming in between the opened drapes awakened Susan about eight o'clock. Her eyes flickered open and moved around the large room, and she noticed for the first time the simple elegance of the heavy oak dresser, bureau, and desk and the inviting softness of the beige carpeting. Throwing back the wine-colored bedspread, she sat up, lowering her feet to the floor, staring with dismay at her skirt and blouse heaped together in an untidy pile on the chair beside the bed. What a sight she was going to be, arriving at the hospital in those wrinkled things! Yet, considering her shameless behavior last night, she decided she was extremely lucky she did not have a problem much more serious than wrinkled clothing this morning. She could have easily awakened to find Adam in bed beside her, and then she really would be in trouble.

Her cheeks growing hot with the mere memory of how she had acted, she stood and went into the bathroom. A few minutes later, as she dressed, she wondered if Adam had gotten up yet to tell his housekeeper she was here. She certainly hoped he had; the idea of walking out and surprising the poor woman did not appeal to her at all. But when she went out down the hall toward the foyer after combing her hair she saw no sign of his housekeeper. As she approached the living room, however, she did hear someone moving around.

"Adam," she called softly, hopefully, as she went down the two steps. Then she nearly stumbled over her own feet when Nellie Brooks rose up out of one of the high-backed chairs that faced toward the fireplace, her expression almost comically astounded as she spun around toward Susan.

"What are you doing in *this* house, so early in the morning?" she asked, her voice high-pitched and harsh. "And where is Mr. Thornton?"

"Uncle Josh is in the hospital," Adam intervened as he came from the direction of the kitchen. "Susan came along when the doctor brought him in."

"I see," Nellie said, inspecting the younger girl with a frown. "So she just decided to spend the night with you?"

"Not exactly. I decided she should stay. We didn't get away from the hospital until four this morning, and since my uncle wants her to be there early today I saw no sense in taking her all the way back to Maiden's Bower."

"I guess I should apologize for barging into this little love nest," Nellie said snidely as her icy gaze swept from Adam to Susan, then back again to him. She jerked the shoulder strap of her purse up over her arm. "But I'm not going to, because I'm not one bit sorry I came. It's been a very enlightening visit. No wonder you were so reluctant to believe me the other day at your uncle's house. After all, the beginning of an affair can dull even an intelligent man's sense of perception." Pausing, she cast an insulting, mocking glance in Susan's direction. "And she's so ambitious that I bet she's willing to do anything you want her to if it'll help her get ahead, won't she?"

"You owe Miss Thomas an apology, Nellie," Adam said softly but emphatically, his eyes gleaming with irritation. "She and I are not having an affair, and I think you know that. And I'd advise you to keep it to yourself that she even stayed part of last night here. Is that understood?"

"Perfectly," the woman snapped back at him as she marched past Susan up the steps into the foyer. Then she stopped short and turned with a flounce of her skirt while a sarcastic smile thinned her lips. "But you know you can't keep this a secret forever, don't you? Soon everybody will know that she's selling and you're buying."

Her heels tapped hard and loud across the foyer's parquet floor, and Adam heaved a disgusted sigh as the front door banged shut. Shaking his head, he smiled apologetically at Susan.

"Well, how does it feel to be branded a scarlet woman?" he asked teasingly. "It looks as if you might be following in Felicity's footsteps in some ways after all."

"Oh, certainly not," she disagreed with a halfhearted smile. "I don't really think Nellie will go around telling this, do you? I mean, since the two of you are . . . well, you know . . . she won't want people to think you're involved with me."

"Are you insinuating Nellie and I are lovers?" he asked softly as he came to her. "Surely you don't believe that?"

"Well, yes, I did think . . . I mean, I just assumed . . ."

"Then you assumed wrong. Nellie and I are business associates, nothing more."

"But does she know that?"

"I've never given her reason to believe otherwise. Besides, she's far more interested in furthering her career than she is in any man."

"I wouldn't be so sure," Susan said skeptically. "She acts as if she owns you, so I don't believe she'll want anybody else to think you're involved with me. She won't tell anyone I spent the night here."

"You don't know her," Adam argued gently, reaching out to brush her hair back across her shoulders. His fingers lingered against her neck, then moved down to trace a disturbing path along her collarbone, visible above the eyelet-embroidered yoke of her white blouse. "If she's interested in me romantically, she'll be jealous enough of you to tell people we spent last night together, just to hurt you."

"But nobody will believe anything happened," Susan said unevenly, gazing up into his dark green eyes, trying not to let his rough fingertips against her skin create too much havoc with her senses. "They'll know nothing happened because your housekeeper was here with us all the time."

"But I lied to you about that, Susan," he admitted with a tender, half-apologetic smile. "I don't really have a live-in housekeeper, but I knew you probably wouldn't stay if I didn't say that I did."

"You mean . . . you mean, nobody else was here?" she stammered, her eyes widening in dismay. "Just the two of us?" When he nodded, she nearly groaned aloud. "Oh, Lord, and I acted so . . . so . . . Oh, I'm really sorry if I made you think I could . . ."

"But I never thought that for a moment," he told her, lifting her chin with one hand so that she had no choice except to look at him. "I realized you were half asleep at first, then everything just got out of hand."

"You're very understanding," she murmured, watching with fascination the firm line of his lips as he smiled.

"Well, to be honest, I do have to admit it's much easier to be understanding now than it was then," he said softly, provocatively. "You certainly didn't make it very easy for me to get to sleep."

Unsurprisingly, Susan blushed. "I'm sorry."

"I'm sorry too, but not especially for that reason. I just regret now that I didn't take you back to Maiden's Bower. If I had, Nellie wouldn't have anything to tell anybody. As it is, I'm afraid you'd better be prepared for some talk about us for a while."

"I promise I won't expect you to marry me, though," Susan said, her eyes softly teasing. "Not even if my reputation's completely ruined."

Smiling slightly, he leaned down to kiss her cheek before releasing her hands. Then he took a step backward, but his eyes never left her face.

"But it doesn't seem very fair, does it?" he asked solemnly. "It seems to me that if we're going to be gossiped about anyway, we may as well really be enjoying a torrid affair."

Though his seemingly serious tone made Susan's breath catch in her throat, she managed to whisper, "Is that a proposition?"

"Maybe," he whispered back. "If it were, would you accept it?"

As Susan looked up at him, she found herself incredibly wavering between wanting to say yes and knowing she should say no. And finally she compromised by giving him no answer at all.

Chapter Seven

Joshua did not get worse, but it took several days for him to actually begin improving. Susan stayed at the hospital much of the time, though there was little she could do except pat his hand comfortingly whenever he called for Meredith or Cathy. However, when the antibiotics Dr. Jenning gave him finally succeeded in reducing his fever and he no longer had periods of delirium, he was concerned about their lack of progress on the Thornton history; so, to placate him, she began working at Maiden's Bower until two or three in the afternoon, then had Baker drive her to the hospital. Still, Joshua was not satisfied with the little progress she was able to make without his collaboration. He became increasingly impatient with Dr. Jennings, who would not let him go home, and only Adam was able to reason with him when he stopped to visit every evening.

After his visit Adam usually took Susan out to dinner, then home. At first she thought it was very pleasant to go out with him for relaxing meals. But after only a few evenings she began to sense a certain tension in his attitude toward her. The reason for that tension remained a mystery until Barbara called her on Tuesday morning, nearly a week after Joshua had entered the hospital.

"There's something I have to tell you," Barbara began mysteriously. Then after a moment's hesitation, she plunged right in. "There's a rumor going around at the Mills agency that you've been chasing after Adam Kincaid, trying to get some choice modeling assignment, *and* that you and he are . . . are having a torrid affair. They're saying it's a known fact that you spent last Wednesday night with him. Now, if that last part's true, it's none of my business. But if it isn't, then I thought you should know what's being said."

Susan groaned. Adam had been right. He had said Nellie would not hesitate to spread her lies around town. After taking a deep shuddering breath, Susan explained the true situation to Barbara.

"Well, I must say that's a relief," Barbara said afterward. "Of course I knew you couldn't be involved with him so he'd help you get a job, but I was a little afraid you might find him attractive enough to . . . to . . ."

"I don't sleep around, Barb," Susan said stiffly. "And you should know that."

Barbara sighed. "I do know that, but . . . Well, I just thought I had to tell you about the rumors."

Susan could not answer. Staring at her hands as they slowly opened and closed, she wished desperately she could get them around Nellie's scrawny neck.

"So what are you going to do about it?" Barbara asked abruptly, rousing Susan from her disturbing thoughts. "Talk to Adam?"

"I really think I'd rather jump off Stone Mountain than talk to him about this. He may already know anyway—he's been a little tense the past two days. Figures, doesn't it? Just when he starts acting as if he can stand me, this has to happen."

"Does it really matter if he can stand you or not?" Barbara asked. "I mean, you didn't seem to care much what he thought of you at first. What's changed your mind?"

"Oh, I don't know exactly. It's just that I'd rather he didn't dislike me."

"And do you like him?" Barbara persisted. "Do you like him as a person?"

"Sometimes," Susan admitted reluctantly. "Much more than I did at first, that's for sure."

"Oh, honey, I think you'd better be very, very careful," Barbara advised softly, ominously. "Don't let yourself like him too much. You don't want to get involved in the kind of game he'd probably want to play."

"I know that," Susan said quietly. "Really I do. I know that."

She meant it too. There was no doubt in her mind that what Barbara believed was true. And she had no intention of forgetting that it was.

Facing Adam that evening was not easy. Luckily, Joshua was feeling much better and he took much of the responsibility for keeping a conversation going, but there was no avoiding the inevitable end of visiting hours. At eight o'clock, as Adam and Susan drove away from the hospital parking lot, she cast occasional cautious glances at his rugged profile, wondering if she should tell him what Barbara had said. Before she could make a decision, however, he was stopping the car, then helping her out, taking her hand as they crossed a busy street to the small restaurant on the other side.

Inside, as they waited to be seated, Susan looked around the dimly lighted room with some surprise. This place was different from the other restaurants they had visited the past few evenings and was certainly in a less fashionable area of town. Yet, despite that, the lack of luxurious trappings here held a certain romantic appeal for her. She liked the small, candlelit tables, the rich, wood-paneled walls, and, especially, the relaxed and hushed atmosphere. Yet, as she and Adam followed the hostess to a table in a secluded corner, she did notice that most of the diners were couples, sitting alone, talking quietly together, sometimes holding hands across the tabletops. Suddenly suspicious of Adam's motive for bringing her here, she had to wonder if he actually had heard the rumors that were circulating about the two of them. Perhaps he had brought her here, where they were less likely to be seen, simply to avoid adding fuel to the gossip.

Inexplicably distressed by that possibility, Susan said very little as she slowly sipped the white wine he had ordered for her.

"You're very quiet tonight," he observed after a few moments of uncomfortable silence. "What is it? Is something wrong?"

"No, nothing," she lied, attempting a cheery smile, too cowardly to tell him what Barbara had heard. "I'm a little tired, that's all."

"You're probably trying to do too much—working most of the day out at the house, then coming to spend hours with Uncle Josh."

"But I don't mind, really I don't. It's not so bad," she began, then halted abruptly when a strikingly attractive woman with auburn hair stopped by Adam's chair and laid a lazy hand on his shoulder.

After glancing up, he immediately pushed back his chair and rose. The newcomer raised herself on tiptoe to kiss his lips lightly.

"Adam, darling, it's so nice to see you," she purred, stroking his lean brown cheek with long, caressing fingers. "Where *have* you been hiding yourself, you rascal? Delia's party last week was an absolute bore without you."

"I haven't been hiding anywhere, Monica," Adam replied. "I've been busy."

"So I've heard," Monica said with a husky, insinuating little laugh as her eyes shifted to Susan. A knowing smile curved her lush, ginger-colored lips.

Susan would not allow herself to fidget nervously under the woman's intent, appraising inspection, though she did feel rather the way she thought the animals in a zoo must feel with people gawking at them.

After Adam made the proper introductions, he glanced around the restaurant curiously. "Where's Bob?" he asked. "I don't see him."

"Bob! Why, you *are* behind the times, aren't you? You shouldn't cut yourself off from your friends this way, really you shouldn't," Monica chided. "If you didn't, you'd know that Bob and I decided we needed a rest from each other, and now we're seeing other people." She turned to wave at a dark-haired, muscular type who was sitting at a side table. "That's Ted," she informed Adam. "I met him at Kate's party a couple of weeks ago, and we've just been inseparable ever since."

"Not exactly pining away for good old Bob, are you?" Adam asked with a wry grin. "And only three months ago, you were absolutely convinced he was *the one*."

"You're making fun of me, I know you are," she accused him with mock indignation. "That's not a very nice thing to do. Can I help it if I'm a little fickle? At least I always *think* I'm in love. I've never had a relationship with any man just because it would be to my advantage. And I steer clear of all the men at the office. *I* certainly wouldn't want to be accused of using sex to get ahead in my career." She bestowed on Susan a rather tight, insincere smile. "I think that sort of thing is just despicable, don't you?"

If her words had been an attempt at veiled sarcasm, Monica had failed miserably. Susan would have had to be incredibly stupid not to recognize the insult in her tone and the disrespectful glitter in her dark eyes. Yet recognizing the slur on her character was one thing; handling it was another. Susan had no idea what to do or say. She sought Adam's eyes, but he was not looking at her. Instead, he was glaring at Monica as if he would dearly love to throttle her pretty, slender neck.

Monica seemed completely unaware of his anger, however, and with a sugary-sweet smile she reached up to straighten his tie.

"Well, it's been fun talking to you, darling, but I really must get back to Teddy. He's so possessive, you know," she said, giggling rather foolishly. "Of course I realize men are always possessive at the beginning of a relationship, but then they get bored as time goes by. Finally they get to the point where they couldn't care less whether you leave them for two hours or two days." She winked conspiratorially at Susan. "Haven't you always found that to be true, dear?"

"You're right, Monica," Adam put in hastily. "Your Teddy seems to be getting a little impatient. You'd better run back over there."

Monica, obviously feeling she had been sufficiently catty, took his advice and scurried away after brushing her lips across his cheek.

"I'm really sorry, Susan," he said softly as he took his seat again. "Monica Bennett can be a very unpleasant person sometimes. But I'm sure you realize from what she insinuated that Nellie's been very busy."

"Yes, well, I knew that anyway," Susan admitted, meeting his surprised look directly. "Barbara, my cousin, told me just this morning that the two of us seem to be the favorite target of the gossipmongers at the Mills agency."

"And that's the real reason you've been so quiet this evening, isn't it?" he asked perceptively. "I can imagine how upsetting this must be to you."

"I *am* trying not to let it upset me too much, since there's absolutely nothing I can do about it." As she tugged nervously at the three-quarter-length sleeves of her plum-colored velour dress, she smiled ruefully. "I do wish Nellie hadn't set out to make me sound like such an ambitious little hussy, though. It wouldn't be nearly so bad if it looked as if I were crazy about you rather than crazy about what you might be able to do for me."

"Even then, it wouldn't be pleasant to know you're being gossiped about."

"But it would be different, much less degrading."

"So you're saying being talked about wouldn't matter that much if you were in love."

"I guess I am. Being in love might make the gossip seem very trivial."

"So I was right about you," Adam said with a teasing smile. "You are a romantic."

"And you think that's foolish?" she inquired seriously, unable for some reason to respond in kind to his mischievous tone. "What's so wrong in being romantic? Why are you such a cynic?"

As the teasing light faded from his green eyes, he shrugged.

"I'm not sure you can call me a cynic. Realistic would be a better word, I think. I've seen too many people like Monica, falling in love at the drop of a hat, then falling out of love just as fast. Almost everybody I know has been divorced once, some of them more than that, and the one thing they all have in common is they started out their marriages in a sort of dreamy, romantic haze that they were sure would last forever. But of course it didn't."

"Maybe they didn't try hard enough to make it last, at least to some degree," Susan offered. "Sometimes I wonder if couples simply give up too easily. A problem comes along that might take some effort to work out, but rather than try to remedy the situation they go their separate ways instead. I think it's sad that they let love die so easily."

"Ah, but maybe it was never really love they felt," he

argued softly yet intensely. "Maybe the kind of love a truly lasting relationship needs is much harder to find than you imagine. I think it must be. I can't think of one married couple I know who act genuinely fond of each other or show any evidence of a willingness to make sacrifices for each other if necessary."

"Has it ever occurred to you that perhaps you're watching the wrong group of people?" she suggested. "Look at the other side. At your own parents, or your uncle and Meredith. And my parents also have something very special together, so it must not be all that rare."

"Maybe this younger generation doesn't know how to find it."

"I think my brother and his wife have found it. And he's a couple of years younger than you are, so how do you explain that?"

"Look, this discussion's very interesting, but we're avoiding the real issue," Adam said evasively. "What we really need to talk about is how to undo some of the damage that's been done to your reputation, if that's possible. First of all, I plan to have a long, long talk with Nellie in the morning. And when I get through with her, she won't be talking about you anymore."

"Nellie probably won't shut up just because you tell her to."

"I think she will when I tell her to either be quiet or find another job," he said calmly. "I know her—she won't take the chance on seeing if I really mean it."

"And will you mean it? Would you really fire her?"

"Yes, I would—and I will if she keeps up this vicious attack on you. She knows everything she's saying is a lie. It's inexcusable, and I want it stopped," he said vehemently, laying his hand over hers on the tabletop. "I would hate for this story to follow you around for the rest of your life. People do have long memories."

That he wanted to protect her pleased Susan more than it should have. She gazed bemusedly at the hand covering hers, then felt bereft somehow when he removed it.

"There is something else we should do," he added then. "Being seen together as we were tonight is just making things worse, so I suggest we avoid each other as much as we can from now on. Don't you agree that would be the wisest thing to do, for your sake?"

"Maybe so," she murmured automatically, bending her head to conceal the bewilderment she was afraid must be showing in her eyes. Perhaps protecting her reputation had nothing to do with this last suggestion. She had not failed to notice the astonishment in Monica Bennett's eyes when she had looked her over. She had been quite surprised that the girl Adam was apparently intimately involved with was such a nondescript little character. Perhaps he had recognized that reaction and decided he would be humiliated by being linked with a girl his friends thought was far beneath his notice.

Adam's suggestion that they avoid each other and Susan's reluctant acceptance turned out to be futile gestures anyway. Joshua Thornton had made different plans, as she discovered the next afternoon.

"Guess what," he said excitedly the moment she walked into his hospital room. "I've talked Dave into letting me go home tomorrow. It wasn't easy, but he finally said I could go if Adam would be willing to ride herd on me." He laughed with some satisfaction. "He seems to think nobody else could handle me, so I told him I'd really make him happy and ask Adam to move in out at the house for a couple of weeks. Then he could really keep an eye on me, and I don't think he'd mind doing it."

Groaning inwardly, Susan gave Joshua a weak smile. If only he knew how very much Adam would mind. . . .

But, to his credit, Adam showed no visible evidence of dismay when he heard his uncle's news that evening. He simply agreed to the plan without even once attempting to exchange a discreet look of disappointment with Susan. Yet his admirably calm acceptance of the inevitable did little to ease her mind.

Chapter Eight

October in the Appalachian foothills was breathtakingly beautiful as the turning leaves attained their peak colors. Brilliant red and orange and softer yellow blanketed the slopes around Maiden's Bower, and Susan could have spent hours gazing out the library window as gentle winds sent increasing numbers of leaves drifting lightly to the ground. Whenever she walked outside, a delicate hint of hickory smoke scented the crisp air. Maiden's Bower and its grounds could quickly make her an impractical dreamer; she realized that fully when she wandered beneath the maple boughs that rustled their orange leaves in the breeze. Walking where nothing much had changed in more than a hundred years invariably sent her imagination spinning into incredible flights of fancy, some of which were infinitely disturbing. Especially now she was able to identify with Felicity Thornton and could imagine her walking these same grounds, feeling a little lost and alone, as she herself sometimes did. Although she did not believe that Adam actually blamed her for the rumors that were circulating, she felt he must harbor at least some resentment, and that made her feel guilty somehow.

Fortunately, Joshua kept her far too busy to wallow excessively in that regret. If he had gotten his way, they would have worked from dawn to midnight on the Thornton history, and only by insisting she needed a walk outside in the fresh air after lunch did she manage to persuade him to rest in his room the hour or so she resolutely stayed away from the library. Yet, though it worried her that he might be trying to do too much too soon, it was difficult to curb his enthusiasm. Whenever she hinted he should go more slowly, her advice only provoked complaints of being a prisoner in his own home, with too many guards telling him what to do.

He was voicing these familiar complaints once again on Wednesday morning, a week after his release from the hospital. Smiling at his grumbling, Susan went to answer the telephone when it rang. To her surprise, the woman on the other end asked for her, then identified herself as Kay Mead, features editor for one of Atlanta's daily newspapers.

"I have your application right here on my desk, Miss Thomas," she said with a certain amount of enthusiasm. "One of my reporters has decided to move elsewhere, so I'll be interviewing applicants early next week. Would you be interested in talking with me? The salary's competitive, as are the fringe benefits."

"It sounds very interesting," Susan replied honestly. "But could you tell me when the job would actually start?"

"Week after next."

"Oh, dear! Well, you see, I've a commitment that will probably last at least two or three more months," Susan explained regretfully. "So I think I'd better just pass this up. But I hope you'll keep me in mind if something similar comes along later," she added hopefully, then bit back a disappointed sigh when the woman informed her that openings in her department came very infrequently. But that could not be helped, and, after she thanked Kay Mead for calling, the conversation ended. As she replaced the receiver, she wondered fleetingly how she had known to reach her here. Then she realized the woman had undoubtedly called Barbara's apartment and been given Joshua's number.

"A job offer?" he asked, watching her closely as she walked across the room to rejoin him. "Tell me all about it."

After she had repeated everything Kay Mead had said to her, he reached out to stroke her hair gently. "But that sounds just like what you were looking for, honey," he reminded her softly. "Don't you think you should at least go talk to her? You could be missing a golden opportunity."

Shaking her head, she smiled at him with real affection. "You know better than to think I'd walk out on you now, with two thirds of this history left to go," she said emphatically. "I promised I'd stay until it's finished and I meant that. There will always be other jobs. And, besides, this is great experience for me too."

"You're the nicest child, did you know that?" he murmured huskily, then cleared his throat with a cough. "And I want you to know I won't forget the sacrifice you've just made for me and my silly old history."

"It's not silly!" she protested, although she was close to tears herself from the look of genuine gratitude she could see in his eyes. "And I'm not making a sacrifice, so just get that idea out of your head. I count myself lucky to be able to help write a history like this, so I don't want to ever hear you say I'm doing *you* a favor again. Now, forget about that job. All right?"

Chuckling now, he lifted his hands acquiescently. "All right, it's forgotten," he promised. "But I still think you're an exceptionally nice child."

Since Joshua kept his promise and did not mention the job offer the rest of the day, Susan too was able to push all thoughts of it to the back of her mind. When Adam came home that evening, however, she began to

wish halfheartedly that her commitment to his uncle
did not also prevent her from separating herself from
him. It was not easy spending most of every evening in
his company, wondering if he would rather be someplace else. But it was not because he ever treated her
unkindly that she felt so uncomfortable around him.
She felt that way because he was nice, much nicer than
she had ever imagined he could be, and his gentleness
toward her did nothing to ease the breathtaking tension
she had always felt around him. It was a tension that
she feared he must recognize, since even the slightest
bit of attention he paid her was capable of bringing a
warm flush of color to her cheeks and a shakiness to her
hands. It was embarrassing, but she did not seem able
to control her reaction.

Joshua was all that saved the evenings from being too
excruciatingly tense. With him there, Susan did not feel
so overwhelmed when Adam spoke to her or smiled her
way. And tonight she was especially grateful for the
older man's light banter, because his nephew looked
more attractive than usual in charcoal-gray slacks and
forest-green crewneck sweater over his shirt. When he
sat down beside her on the sofa and draped his arm
across the sofa back, the faint spicy fragrance of his
aftershave reminded her of the kisses they had shared,
which did nothing to calm her nerves. Every muscle in
her body seemed to tighten painfully as his hard, lean
thigh brushed against hers, but she was reasonably sure
she had masked that reaction by turning nonchalantly
toward Joshua when he spoke again.

"This time of year always reminds me of the Harvest
Ball Meredith and I used to give," he said with a
reminiscent smile. "It's hard to believe the last one
was nineteen years ago. You remember that one,
don't you, Adam? The one before . . . before Cathy
died?"

"I remember," Adam said softly. Then he leaned
slightly forward toward Susan to grin at his uncle. "Isn't

that the one when Maggie Jerome came dressed as Marie Antoinette and her wig fell off into the spiked punch?"

"It sure was, and I've always suspected she'd been doing a lot of dipping into that punch before that happened. I'm not sure she ever really noticed it had fallen off." Joshua laughed softly, remembering. "Though I think most of the men could have throttled her for ruining all that fine whiskey."

"It was more whiskey than punch," his nephew commented wryly. "I'll never forget my first taste of it. I was fifteen and tired of having to drink that pink lemonade stuff in the bowl at the opposite end of the table. But I was glad enough to get some of it after nearly burning up my throat with your concoction."

"I never knew you gave Harvest Balls, Mr. Thornton," Susan spoke up. "I thought they stopped after your grandparents died."

"Oh, no, my parents carried on with it, then Meredith and I did too until nineteen years ago," Joshua told her with a sigh. "After that last one, we just didn't feel up to arranging any more. But, you know, now I really regret that we didn't. I think Cathy would have wanted us to."

"Why don't you consider holding one this year?" Adam suggested abruptly. "There are still a great many people around here who would love to come to one again."

"You think they would, really?" his uncle asked, his eyes lighting up in a way Susan had never seen before. But then his hopeful smile faded. "Oh, it's silly to even think of doing it. That stick-in-the-mud Dave Jennings would never even hear of letting me plan something like that."

"He might if you promised to leave most of the planning to Susan and me—that is, if she'd be willing to do it. Would you, Susan?"

"Of c-course," she stammered, shocked that he

would actually suggest something that would necessitate their being together more than they already had to be. Yet it was not an unpleasant shock, she realized with some dismay, knowing she was a fool to feel elated that he had suggested it. But she was, and it took all her inate honesty to compel her to admit she had no experience in planning a large party, much less a huge costume ball. "I wouldn't even know where to begin," she concluded.

"No problem," Joshua assured her, bubbling with enthusiasm now. "I still have the guest list Meredith revised every year, and of course we'd hire a caterer. Plus some of the high-school kids around here would be glad to put up the decorations if you just wanted to supervise."

"Great idea," Adam agreed, brushing his fingers across her shoulder persuasively. "And I really would take half the responsibility—I wouldn't leave all the work to you."

"I know that," she murmured, catching her breath at the smile he suddenly gave her. She smiled back nervously. "Oh, all right, I'll give it a try. But don't blame me if everything's a complete disaster."

"It won't be," he said with supreme confidence. Then he turned his attention back to his uncle. "How about that guest list, Uncle Josh? If it's somewhere handy, why don't we take a look at it now?"

Nothing could have pleased Joshua more. After getting the list from the oak secretary, the three of them started going through it, Susan revising as they told her which names to omit and also added a few new ones. They became so engrossed in their task that when the grandfather clock struck ten they were surprised it was that late.

"Maybe you should go on up to bed, Uncle Josh," Adam suggested worriedly. We can't have you wearing yourself out doing this."

"But I don't want to be left out completely," his

uncle muttered petulantly. "I'm not dead yet, you know."

"We have no intentions of leaving you out," Adam answered patiently. "We won't omit or add another name until tomorrow night when you can help us. You'll *have* to help because I don't even remember some of these names."

Obviously mollified, Joshua got slowly to his feet, then smiled rather sheepishly down at them. "Sorry I bit your head off," he said earnestly. "Maybe I won't be such a grump after a good night's sleep."

After watching him walk out the door and close it behind him, Susan turned to Adam, gesturing uncertainly. "Do you really think he's up to all this?" she asked with real concern. "It's going to be quite an undertaking."

"I think it'll do him a world of good," was Adam's answer. Then he smiled gently. "It's been nineteen years since I've seen him as excited as he was when we started going over that list."

"But there are so many names here. Are you sure having so many people won't get him too excited?"

Adam's hand came up to lift a strand of hair off her shoulder as his dark gaze held hers. "We can't protect him so much that he does nothing but sit around all day, Susan. What kind of life would that be?"

"Not a very pleasant one," she conceded, smiling apologetically. "You're right. I just didn't think of it that way, I guess."

As he smiled at her, Susan felt a sudden, intense stab of regret that she had become such an irritant in his life. He was really very nice. Impulsively, she laid her hand on his forearm.

"Oh, Adam, I'm so sorry about all this mess, really I am," she said urgently. "I know it must be embarrassing to face all your friends now, knowing they think you . . . you and I . . .,"

His narrowed eyes scanned her face. "Embarrassing?

For me? I'm afraid I don't know what you mean exactly."

Unable to meet his puzzled gaze, she stared out across the library. "You don't have to put on an act for my sake, really. I saw the way your friend Monica looked at me the other evening. She couldn't believe you'd gotten yourself involved with somebody as unexciting as I am."

"You really are very young, aren't you, Susan?" he asked softly after a moment. Grasping her jaw in exquisitely gentle fingers, he turned her head toward him. "Why in the world would you think I wouldn't want my friends to believe I was involved with you?"

"Because I'm n-nothing like the women y-you usually get involved with," she answered haltingly, trying to ignore the shiver of anticipation that slid along her spine as his fingers on her cheek became caressing. She tried to turn her face away as they moved closer and closer to her lips. "That's why you said we should avoid being seen together; I know that."

"You know nothing," he whispered chidingly. "Not if you couldn't see that what Monica was feeling the other night was envy rather than contempt."

"Envy?" she exclaimed softly. "Why should she envy me? Unless she's interested in you herself. Is that it?"

"No, that isn't it. She was envious, I imagine, because she can't understand how you manage to keep that innocent look when, according to Nellie, you are more than a little experienced. Monica knows that would be an inconsistency many men would find nearly irresistible."

"Many men, but not you?" Susan was compelled to ask. Then she frowned slightly as he gave her an indulgent smile.

"But *I* know you really are just as innocent as you look, remember? Your appearance and your actions aren't inconsistent to me."

"Just boring," she muttered somewhat bitterly, staring at the smooth brown skin visible where his collar was open. "Isn't that what you're saying?"

"Why do you always insist on putting words into my mouth?" he asked, more than a hint of anger in his voice as he jerked her chin up. "And how could I ever be bored around you when all you ever do is provoke me?"

"I do not."

"Yes you do!" he whispered, gripping her upper arms. "You can provoke me just by looking at me as if you want me to kiss you, then getting all wide-eyed and reproachful if I need to do more than simply kiss."

"I just don't know *how* to act around you!"

"Don't act at all," he answered wearily, his anger abating now. "Just be yourself—innocent, small-town Susan."

"And completely unresponsive to you?" She sighed unhappily, determined to be honest. "Innocent doesn't mean frigid, Adam. It just means inexperienced. It doesn't mean I wouldn't like you to . . ." Her words trailed off to breathless silence as his narrowed eyes darkened to deeper green and his hands slid from her arms across her shoulders to tangle in the silky strands of her hair. Half expecting a violent reaction, she was not prepared for the assault that gentleness made on her senses. When he bent his head down, seeking the smooth skin of her throat with his mouth, she clenched her fists, digging her fingernails into her palms to keep from moaning softly.

But resistance was not what he wanted from her now.

"Oh, relax!" he coaxed urgently, opening her mouth slightly with the edge of his thumb. "Let me really kiss you!"

And the warmth of his hard lips playing with hers melted away all Susan's resolve to remain unresponsive. Before she could control them, her hands slid beneath his sweater over the taut muscles of his back as his mouth took complete possession of hers. Then, somehow, they were lying in each other's arms on the long, wide sofa and Adam was slowly lowering the back zipper of her dress. The evocative pressure of his hard thighs against her own was a compelling inducement she could not resist. She murmured contentedly when he pushed the soft jersey fabric from her shoulder to seek the creamy softness of her skin with his lips.

"I *need* you!" he muttered hoarsely, lifting his head to gaze down at her. "Don't you realize that? What would you do if I didn't want to let you go until . . . Would you stop me?"

"I wouldn't want to," she whispered honestly, stroking his cheek with trembling fingers when he took a sharp breath. "I'm not even sure I could try."

"Susan, you're driving me crazy," he exclaimed softly before kissing her again with nearly bruising force. But then he released her mouth reluctantly. "And what would you do if I made you pregnant?"

"Oh, Adam, I don't know. I've never thought of what I might do if that ever happened."

"Maybe you better start thinking about it, then, because every time I touch you it becomes more of a possibility. And I don't want to hurt you the way Jonathan hurt Felicity."

"I've told you I wouldn't expect marriage if I ever let that happen. I'd have options Felicity never had."

"And what would you do?" he asked gently but skeptically. "Would you have an abortion? Or go off somewhere and have the baby, then just give it away?" Smiling knowingly, he shook his head as his fingertips traced a disturbing path along her cheek. "You couldn't do either of those things, and I'd never let you anyway."

"Why wouldn't you?" she asked breathlessly, an incongruous hope building in her, a hope that he would give a reason she had no right to expect. "Tell me why."

"Because I could never let you face something like that alone," he said candidly. "I'm not irresponsible, Susan. I'm fond enough of you that I'd want to take care of you and the child. But that wouldn't be enough for you, would it? You want an all-consuming love."

"Yes, that's what I want," she admitted, chewing her lip unhappily as she gazed up into the darkness of his eyes. "And you don't believe such a thing even exists, I know that."

With a heavy sigh Adam sat up beside her, but his hands lingered disturbingly around her slender waist.

"I should never have come out here to stay," he said quietly. "I was afraid we'd just get more involved than we already were. It can't go on this way, Susan. Either I don't touch you at all, or I . . . But I think it's getting to the point where you'll have to be the one who makes that decision, because I can't seem to stop myself from touching you. You may have to do the stopping now."

"That's not very fair," she muttered, closing her eyes, hating herself for wanting to cry. "Whatever happened to all that talk about ending the double standard? I thought modern society had tossed out that old rule about girls being responsible for saying no."

"But you don't really fit in such a modern world, do you?" he said very seriously. "So the new rules don't apply." Releasing her then, he took a cigarette from the box on the side table and lit it. "Look, I'm just trying to warn you that you might not be able to count on me to stop next time. There's a limit, you know."

She certainly did know, because her emotions had just reached it. Not sure what to say or do, she sat up, then buried her face in the arm she draped across the back of the sofa. And when Adam's hand moved soothingly over her shoulders, she tensed.

"Are you crying?" he asked gently. When she shook

her head, he took her arm to turn her around. "But you are upset."

"I'm just tired," she lied, but her words sounded dreadfully unconvincing even to herself. "I think I'll go to bed now."

Nodding, he touched her cheek with gentle fingertips as his dark eyes moved slowly over her face. "You're a very intriguing person," he murmured. "Sometimes I wish . . ."

She waited, her heart beating a little faster as a result of his unusually indecisive tone of voice, but he did not finish what he had begun to say. Fighting her disappointment, she gave him a wan little smile, but after she swung her feet to the floor he prevented her from standing by curving his large hands around her waist.

"I'm sorry all this confusion's making you so unhappy."

Unable to answer, she only nodded, then scurried to her feet the moment he released her and hurried out the door. As she trudged up the stairs, she pressed her fingers against her lips, wishing he had been right in thinking it was confusion that was making her so unhappy. But he was wrong—she had stopped being confused about her feelings toward him about fifteen minutes ago. Now she was sure she cared about him as she had never cared about another person in her life. And it was that certainty, not confusion, that was making her so miserable.

After a ridiculously restless night, then getting out of bed with what seemed to be the beginning of a cold, Susan felt terrible the next morning. For once, she had little enthusiasm to put into her work and left it to Joshua to tell her what he wanted to do without making any suggestions of her own. Even when he cast her curious glances, she could not muster the energy to pretend that nothing was bothering her. Finally, about

eleven o'clock he sighed and laid aside the typed pages
he was proofreading.

"What's the matter, honey?" he asked worriedly.
"You're looking mighty pale today."

"I think I must be catching cold," she told him. "I've
been sneezing and my throat feels a little scratchy."

"Then why didn't you tell me you felt too bad to
work?" he asked with uncharacteristic impatience,
getting up to come lay his hand against her forehead.
"You do feel a little warm. Now, I want you to stop
what you're doing and go straight up to your room to lie
down for the rest of the day. I don't want you getting
really sick."

His genuine concern and the general malaise she felt
combined to make her eyes fill with tears. "You're so
nice to me," she muttered thickly. Then, shaking her
head, she controlled her overwrought emotions. "But I
really don't feel bad enough to go to bed. Let's get back
to work."

"No. If you refuse to go to bed, then I insist you at
least sit over here on the sofa and relax until it's time
for lunch. We can have a nice chat."

The soft sofa cushions did look very inviting, so she
did not protest when Joshua took her arm and impelled
her gently across the room. Then, as he shared some of
his ideas about the upcoming ball, she tried to make
herself more comfortable by tucking a throw pillow
against the dull ache in the small of her back. It did not
help much and within a few minutes she was moving
restlessly, unable to settle herself in a position to ease
all the aches that were now spreading down her arms
and legs. Yet, despite her discomfort, she tried to pay
attention to what Joshua was saying about the ball.

"You know, of course, I want you to feel free to
invite anybody you want," he was saying. "If there's a
young man from home you'd like to have come, I'd be
glad to put him up here at the house."

She smiled gratefully. "That's a very kind offer, really. But I can't think of any young man I'd like to invite."

He eyed her suspiciously. "Come on now, honey. Don't try to tell me there's not some special person in your life. Why, you're so pretty I bet you had all the boys in town camped out on your doorstep."

"I wasn't quite that popular, but I suppose I did have my share of dates," she told him. "But I still can't think of anybody I want to invite to the ball."

"Really? Are you sure?"

"I would like to invite my cousin Barbara to the ball," she said with the only real enthusiasm she had felt all morning. "I know she'd love to wear some really exotic costume. Besides, I'd like you to meet her. I think I'll call her right now, if that's okay?"

"Go right ahead. And while you do that, I think I'll take a short walk outside. Maybe the fresh air will improve my appetite."

Luckily, Barbara was home, and the invitation to the ball was met with a squeal of delight. "Oh, what will I wear?" she exclaimed excitedly. "What are *you* going to wear?"

"I don't know yet; I haven't had time to think," Susan told her. "We just decided last night to have the ball."

"When is it? How much time do I have to find a really fabulous costume?"

"Joshua decided on the first Saturday night in November."

"Oh, no, you're kidding!" Barbara groaned. "Darn it all! Wouldn't you know my very first out-of-town assignment is that very same weekend. I won't be able to come, and it would have been so much fun. Isn't it just awful?"

"Yes, awful," Susan muttered in agreement, disappointment washing over her. "I wanted so much for you to come and keep me company. I'm not going to have much fun now, either, since I won't know anybody, really."

"Sure you will. Adam Kincaid will be there, won't he?" Barbara asked, her tone suggestive. "You *must* know him since the two of you are living in the same house now."

"So you've heard about that already?"

"Honey, I heard about that several days ago."

"They're still talking about us as much as they were then?"

"Well, no, not quite as much," Barbara conceded, then added reassuringly: "Don't let it worry you too much anyway. They'll find somebody else to gossip about pretty soon now."

"If you say so," Susan answered dejectedly, then changed the subject. "Where are you going on this assignment?"

"Bermuda! Can you believe it?" Barbara squealed. "There are four of us going for a three-day weekend. Of course, I doubt we'll have much time to do anything on our own, especially if that old battle-ax Nellie Brooks comes along to keep her eye on things. Really, I . . ."

As her cousin rambled on and on, Susan sneezed several times. Finally, Barbara halted midsentence. "You sound just awful. You'd better do something about that cold."

"Oh, I'll be all right."

"Is that why you sound so down this morning?"

"Maybe that's part of it," Susan said tiredly. "I guess it is."

"Are you sure that's all of it, though?" her cousin persisted. "You haven't gotten yourself more involved with Mr. Kincaid, have you?" When Susan was unable to lie and simply left the question unanswered for a long moment, Barbara exclaimed: "You have, haven't you? That's what you've done! Oh, Susan, didn't I warn you? How involved?"

Susan took a long, tremulous breath, then lowered her voice to a near whisper: "I think I'm in love with him."

"Maybe it's just infatuation," Barbara argued hopefully. "After all, he's older than you and more sophisticated than anybody you've ever been interested in before. Maybe you just think you love him."

"I hope so," Susan said emotionally. "If I don't get over this silliness soon I'm going to start wishing I'd gone for that interview with that Mead woman."

"What Mead woman?"

"You know, the features editor from the newspaper. She called you and you gave her my number out here."

"I haven't given anybody your number," Barbara informed her, her tone confused. "Nobody from any newspaper's called here about you."

"But somebody must have! How else would she have known to reach me here? Your number's the one I put on all the applications. I never even knew Joshua then! It doesn't make sense. Are you positive nobody's called? Maybe it just slipped your mind."

"That kind of call wouldn't slip my mind, and you know it," Barbara protested. "Besides, what's the big deal? Somebody else must have given that woman your number out there."

"But who could have? I can't think . . ." Susan's words halted abruptly as she finally realized that Barbara had not given Kay Mead her number. Perhaps it meant that Adam had had something to do with the editor's call. And she had imagined he was beginning to trust her! Suddenly the aching in her head became a sharp, stabbing pain in her temples. Without delay, she told Barbara she had to go and hung up the phone to burrow her face into her folded arms on the desk. Why had Adam found it necessary to test her? Surely he knew by now that she was not going to leave Joshua until his family history was finished.

"Oh, darn," she mumbled miserably. Then she sat

up straight as a far more disturbing thought occurred to her. Maybe Adam had not been testing her at all. Maybe he had persuaded Kay Mead to consider her for that job, hoping she would take it if it were offered. That way, he would be rid of her once and for all. She moaned softly. That possiblity was so devastating that now she really did feel ill.

Chapter Nine

The weather turned unseasonably cold and rainy, and Susan caught a cold that got worse instead of better. By Thursday night she felt so terrible she could not eat anything for dinner. It took all her energy simply to remain sitting up in her dining-room chair as Adam and Joshua had their meal. Every part of her ached and she had developed a deep cough that sounded as if she were ready to be confined in a tuberculosis sanatorium.

Occasionally during dinner she sensed Adam's eyes on her, but she refused to look up at him. After all, he was partly responsible for how lousy she felt; it would serve him right if he worried a little about her now. With a quiet sniffle, she blinked back the tears of weakness that suddenly filled her eyes as she pushed her food around on her plate with her fork.

After what seemed an interminable time, dinner was over. Preceding Joshua and Adam, Susan dragged her feet as she went into the library; but as soon as she sat down on the sofa she knew she could no longer pretend to be feeling all right. A few more minutes and she was afraid she would no longer be able to hold up her head. She stood, swaying slightly on weak, trembling legs, and smiled apologetically at Joshua.

"I'm not feeling at all well," she whispered, her voice

hoarse from coughing. "I think I'd better go lie down. Do you mind?"

"Of course not! Go on," he insisted worriedly. "Maybe I should call Dave Jennings over here to have a look at you."

"Oh, no, that won't be necessary," she said as she walked toward the door. "I'm sure I'll feel much better tomorrow."

"Susan, wait a moment!" Adam called after her as she reached the open door. Then he hurried to her, frowning as she hung on weakly to the doorjamb. "You look like you feel horrible."

"I guess I do," she admitted, tears filling her already fever-bright eyes as she looked up at him. "I just need to go to bed."

"Are you sure? That cough sounds very bad to me." He pressed the back of his hand gently against her cheek, then took a sharp, dismayed breath as she covered his hand with her own, not wanting to lose the coolness of his skin against the excessive heat of hers. "Good Lord, you're burning up! Are you sure we shouldn't call Dave?"

"Well, I do have this awful pain," she admitted, pressing her fingers into the hollow between her breasts. "It really hurts."

"I'm calling him right now," he said urgently. But before he could move away, Susan was reaching out to him. Her heart was pounding furiously, making her dizzy, and just before a silent darkness blocked out everything, she felt Adam's strong arms go around her, lifting her up safe against his chest.

When she opened her eyes, she was on the bed in her own room and Dr. Jennings was bending over her. "I don't feel very well," she told him unnecessarily. "I ache all over."

"Most people with pneumonia do," he retorted with mock severity as he held her wrist between his fingers.

"It's a good thing you fainted, young lady. A day or two more of this and you could have been in pretty bad shape. Pneumonia's something nobody can afford to play around with."

"But I didn't know I had it."

"How could you? You didn't come to see me so I could tell you."

Too tired to talk or even keep her eyes open, she shut them again and didn't know anything else until Dr. Jennings started calling her name softly.

"Susan, lie still now while I give you this injection of penicillin."

Even the word injection could not rouse her and she barely felt the stinging prick of her skin. All she wanted to do was go to sleep, but first she had to sit up a bit and swallow two pills. She lay back down, snuggling her cheek against the softness of the pillow, and when gentle hands adjusted the covers around her she murmured her gratitude without opening her eyes.

The narcotic Dr. Jennings gave her eased the pain in her chest and controlled her cough but also kept her in a hazy world of semiconsciousness for the next two days. It was impossible to distinguish between dream and reality. Sometimes she was a child again, following her brother and his friends through the woods near their house, feeling lonely and left out when they managed to escape her. Other times she was with Adam and he was being nice to her, holding her gently, making her feel secure and happy. There were only a few lucid moments, when Emily would help her sit up to take her medicine or sip broth from a mug, that she realized most of what she had thought was real had only been dreams.

The first time she really awoke fully was late Saturday afternoon when the bright autumn sun was filtering around the edges of the closed yellow drapes. For a moment she simply lay still, adjusting her eyes to the light, realizing as she took a deep breath that the pain in her chest was mercifully gone. Turning her head on the pillow then, she half gasped at the sight of Adam, sitting in the chair beside the bed, his eyes closed as he rested his head against the wing. She called his name softly, smiling rather shyly at him when his eyes opened immediately and he sat up straight.

"How do you feel?" he asked gently, leaning forward to rest his elbows on his knees. "Dave said you'd be waking up completely this afternoon since he didn't need to give you any more codeine."

"So that's what made me feel so odd. I'd try to wake up but somehow I couldn't. It's hard to believe I slept all last night and all today too."

Adam shook his head, his expression irresistibly tender. "It's Saturday, Susan, not Friday."

"Really?" she exclaimed, grimacing as she clutched her hands around her head. "Oh, I must look hideous. I bet my hair is an awful mess."

"You look just fine," he assured her with an indulgent smile. "Emily's been keeping your hair brushed. And I even brushed it myself, once."

Susan's eyes widened in amazement.

"You did? Well . . . I . . . th-thank you," she stammered, drawing up the bedclothes close under her chin without being aware she was doing it. "W-were you here with me often?"

"Whenever I could, I gave Emily a break."

"Oh. Oh, I see. It was very nice of you to help her."

Perhaps Adam detected the hint of disappointment in her tone, because he got up from the chair, then sat down on the edge of the bed, taking both her hands in his.

"I didn't stay with you just to help Emily," he said softly, sincerely. "I was worried about you—you've been a very sick girl, almost delirious at times."

"Almost delirious?" she exclaimed fearfully, wondering what humiliating secrets she might have revealed. "You mean I talked sometimes?"

"A couple of times."

"Wh-what did I say?"

"Does it matter?"

Susan closed her eyes briefly. If he was reluctant to tell her what she had said, it must be because he knew she'd be embarrassed. But she had to know!

"I wish you'd tell me," she whispered, glancing at him for only a moment before staring past him out into the room. "Please."

"All right, I'll tell you—if you tell me who the hell Bill is."

"Bill? He's my brother," she said, bewildered by the hint of inexplicable anger she had detected in his voice. "Why do you want to know?"

Raking his fingers through the thick silvery hair that swept across his forehead, he sighed and shook his head. "I just wondered—you said his name several times, almost as if you were calling for him. I think you were dreaming."

"Oh, yes, I remember now," she said, able to breathe again until she also recalled vaguely some of the dreams she had had about Adam. Her eyes darted up to meet his. "D-did I say anybody else's name?" When he only nodded as his dark, unreadable gaze drifted over her face, then lingered on the soft, inviting fullness of her mouth, her entire body became as warm as her cheeks already were. "Whose name?" she whispered breathlessly. "Who else did I call for?"

He smiled then.

"You said my name a few times. But I'm not sure if you were dreaming or actually knew I was here. *Did* you dream about me, Susan?"

"I can't remember," she lied, then caught her breath sharply as he laid caressing fingertips into the appealing hollow at the base of her throat and the heel of his hand rested heavily on the firm, full curve of her breast.

"Do you know you manage to look desirable even in that ridiculous flannel nightgown?" he murmured, then shook his head with a gently mocking smile as her eyes widened. "But I'm not going to attack you, so you needn't look so scared."

"I'm not scared," she protested, her blush deepening. "It's just a little embarrassing, knowing you've been here so much when I was asleep."

As he took his hand away, his jaw tightened. "I'm not a barbarian, Susan," he said impatiently. "It never even occurred to me that we were alone in a bedroom. I wasn't tempted once to take advantage of you."

"Oh, but I didn't mean it that way! Really, I didn't!" Reaching up, she touched his cheek. "I know you wouldn't . . . I know that!"

Taking her hand, he lowered it back to the bed as he stood. "You should rest now."

"But, Adam, don't be angry. I didn't mean . . ." Her words trailed off as he turned and walked toward the door, and when he stopped to look back for a moment, she could not find the right words to begin again. Then he was gone. With a weak exclamation of pure frustration, she turned over onto her side to rub her cheek against the pillow. She was feeling better, but other than that nothing had changed. No matter what she did or what she said, she somehow managed to antagonize him.

By Monday morning, Susan was feeling well enough to get out of bed and go back downstairs to work. She was feeling well enough but she was not allowed to do it. Dr. Jennings flatly refused to even consider letting her leave her room until Tuesday evening, when she could dress and go down for dinner, but not to work.

"But I'm so bored!" she told him. "I can't read all the time. I need something else to do."

"Can you knit?" the doctor asked without smiling as he tucked his stethoscope back into his bag. "Maybe this would be a good time to start making Christmas presents."

"I don't want to knit. Not when I know how much work there is to do with this ball coming up."

"As far as I know, Adam's handling all the arrangements very nicely."

"But it's not fair for him to have to," she argued as she rebuttoned the yoke of her gown. "I promised him I'd help."

David Jennings shook his head at her. "You're just looking for excuses to get out of this room. You know very well that Adam understands you can't help him if you're sick."

"But I'm not sick anymore."

"Hmmph. You're weak as a baby. You just don't realize it because you haven't really exerted yourself. A couple of hours downstairs working and you'd be glad to come crawl back into bed."

"Oh, I don't feel that weak. Couldn't I just try it tomorrow? I really feel bad about holding Mr. Thornton up on his history."

Dr. Jennings shook his finger at her, but there was a hint of an amused gleam in his eyes.

"Listen, I really don't need a difficult patient," he began, then stopped as somebody knocked on the door. And when Joshua peeked inside the room, he beckoned him in. "Come on in. Maybe you can talk some sense into this stubborn young lady. Tell her pneumonia is not something you bounce back from quickly."

"He's right, honey," Joshua said, giving her a comforting smile. "You can't try to do too much too soon or you might make yourself very sick again."

"But I promise I'll try to take it easy," Susan said, her hopeful gaze going from Joshua to the doctor, then back again. "Couldn't we work at least a couple of hours on the history every day? And a little while on the arrangements for the ball?"

"Absolutely not," Dr. Jennings said sternly, picking up his jacket from the bedside chair. "And I don't want to hear another word about it for the rest of this week. Next Monday, maybe I'll let you start working a few hours every day."

The no-nonsense gleam in his eyes convinced her that arguing was getting her nowhere and never would. With a disgruntled sigh, she slumped back against the headboard of the bed.

"Oh, it won't be as long a week as you think," Joshua said consolingly a moment later after Dr. Jennings had left. "Besides, I've got a surprise for you that might make playing the invalid a little more glamorous anyway." Smiling secretively, he went to the door, opened it, then reached down for something out in the hall. It was a gold-foil-wrapped package sporting a large white bow, which he handed to her with a flourish and a stiff bow from the waist.

"You didn't have to do this," she murmured as she examined the gaily wrapped box. "But I'm glad you did." Smiling happily as he laughed, she slipped the crisscrossed ribbons off the box, then carefully removed the paper. But after lifting off the lid of the box and opening the tissue paper, she gasped with wonder as she carefully unfolded an exquisite satin and lace bedjacket and the gown beneath it. "Oh, they're just beautiful!" she whispered. "I've never seen anything like them."

"I bought them where Meredith always shopped for her lingerie. She said nothing could cheer a sick woman like a beautiful, impractical nightgown."

"I think she was right," Susan said softly, stroking the smooth, pale plum-colored satin with the tips of her fingers. Then she held up the gown to get a better look, realizing only then just how elegant it was in its simplicity. Unembellished even by lace, it had a low v-neck bodice supported by dainty spaghetti-string straps, and the figure-hugging floor-length skirt flared out gently at the hem. It was a provocative garment that could be made demure simply by adding the fitted lace and satin bedjacket, and Susan loved it. But knowing how incredibly expensive it must have been, she shook her head at Joshua. "You really shouldn't have done it. I love it, but you shouldn't have."

"And why not?" he asked defensively. "I wanted to get you something pretty, and when the girl at the shop showed me this I knew I had to get it. It's just the right color to go with those eyes of yours and your hair."

"But still . . ."

"Surely you don't think it's an inappropriate gift?" he interrupted with a mischievous grin. "Old as I am, you can't believe I have any ulterior motive for giving you a present like this. I just thought you deserved something beautiful."

"Thank you," she said softly, smiling up at him as he patted her shoulder. "I can't wait to try it on. I'm sure it will fit, though. Six is my size. And, by the way, how *did* you know what size to buy?"

"Emily helped me there," he told her. And, after she took it and squeezed his hand with a murmured thank you, he gestured toward the door. "I'm going to rest awhile and give you a chance to try that on. Do you think you'll need Emily to help you?"

"No, I'll be fine," she said, watching him walk to the door. "But wait," she called, smiling as he turned around. "Getting this really has made me feel guilty that I can't be doing my part to get ready for the ball. Couldn't I at least address the invitations while I'm stuck up here?"

"Well, now, that doesn't sound very strenuous, does it?" he agreed. "Tell you what, I'll call Dave this afternoon and see what he has to say about that idea."

After he had left, Susan got eagerly out of the bed to slip off the flannel gown she had on and replace it with the new one. The effect was more than satisfactory, she realized when she looked in the mirror. The color did suit her, and the smooth satin clung to the curves of her body. For once she looked sophisticated, at least a little bit, and she was smiling to herself as she sat back down on the edge of the bed.

But Susan's self-satisfied feeling faded abruptly that evening when Joshua visited her again after dinner.

"I'm afraid we'll have to drop the idea of you addressing the invitations," he informed her. "I'm sorry."

"But since I'd be doing them up here, sitting in bed or in the chair, I can't see why Dr. Jennings won't let me do them!"

"Oh, it isn't Dave who doesn't want you to," Joshua said surprisingly. "He said it would be okay. It's Adam who thinks you'll tire yourself too much. He says he won't allow it."

"*He* won't allow it?" Susan exclaimed, suddenly very angry. Why did Adam care whether she did too much or didn't? She had only seen him twice since Saturday evening, and both those times he had only leaned his head inside the door to say hello. Now, after ignoring her for two whole days, he had the nerve to sit downstairs and issue orders concerning what she could or could not do. Tyrant! That's what he was, and she would not stand for it!

"You tell Adam for me that I'll do the invitations anyway since you and Dr. Jennings think it will be all right," she told Joshua stiffly. "You tell him what I do is none of his business."

Joshua stared at her disbelievingly for a moment, then shook his head. "Are you sure you want me to tell him those exact words, honey?"

"Of course. Why not? That's what I said, isn't it?"

"Well, yes, but you're being a little bit harsh, don't you think?" he asked bewilderedly.

"And he's being a little bossy, don't *you* think?"

"That's not the way he meant it, I'm sure. Adam's just very direct."

"Well, I don't like it. And you can tell him that too. He's not going to ignore me for days, then start ordering me around."

Something like amusement seemed to flicker in Joshua's blue eyes, but he kept a straight face as he stood. "All right, I'll tell him, but I'll have to wait until morning. I think he's probably already gone out for the evening."

"In the morning will be fine," she muttered petulantly, ignoring the relief she suddenly felt when she heard that Adam was not downstairs. She lifted her chin defiantly. "Then, after you tell him, have Emily bring up the invitations and the list, if you wouldn't mind. I'll get to work on them right away."

With a smile now definitely tugging at the corners of his mouth Joshua nodded as he turned to go out.

When the door closed behind him, Susan sank back against the headboard, her entire body tense and hot as a result of that flare-up of temper. It had been silly and childish to get so upset, she decided regretfully, but Adam had always been adept at arousing the most violent emotions in her, and his ability to do so seemed to be strengthening with every day that passed. She was tired of letting him bother her. She loved him and he did nothing but reject her and she was getting increasingly angry at herself for letting him hurt her. She was not going to let him do it anymore, she resolved, closing her eyes wearily. But they opened again almost immediately when the door suddenly swung open.

"Adam! I thought you'd gone out!" she said, folding her arms instinctively across her chest as her eyes widened at the expression on his face. "M-Mr. Thornton told me you were going."

"But I hadn't left yet," he said, his deep voice deceptively soft. "And since I was still here, he gave me your message."

"Did he?" she asked, her voice revealingly strained and squeaky.

"He certainly did." Coming to stand by the bed, he looked down at her. "He told me every word."

"Oh," she breathed, unable to tear her fascinated gaze from the hard, tight line of his jaw. Then, with great effort, she remembered her firm resolution. She made herself shrug. "I suppose you're mad about what I said, but I'm afraid I don't much care if you are. You should know I'm going batty cooped up in this room, but you won't *allow* me to address a few invitations to the ball. Why? Have you decided you don't want me to help with the arrangements?"

Thrusting his hands deep into his trouser pockets, he sighed impatiently. "You're being ridiculous, Susan. And you know you are. Why shouldn't I want you to help with the arrangements?"

"You know why—because you don't want to spend any more time with me than you absolutely have to," she answered bluntly. "What you've seemed to forget is that I'd be addressing them up here in my room. You wouldn't have to have a thing to do with me."

"Oh, for heaven's sake, be quiet!" he commanded harshly, reaching out to encircle her neck with one large, strong hand. "You get the silliest ideas in your head and I'm sick and tired of hearing them."

"Why don't you go ahead and finish that statement?" she asked bitterly, glaring up at him. "Be honest for once—just say it! Say you're sick and tired of everything about me, because I know you are. You've always been."

"Stop it, Susan!" he whispered furiously, increasing the pressure of his fingers against the smooth skin of her throat. "I have no idea what brought this little tantrum on, but enough is enough. I am not trying to leave you out of making the arrangements. I simply didn't want you working until you've had enough time to get completely well."

"I don't believe that for a minute," she muttered, reaching up, trying to pry his fingers from around her neck. But after only a few seconds of futile struggling, she realized how very weak she still was. As her heart pounded from the exertion and her hands dropped down limply at her sides, she whispered: "Stop lying, please. I know exactly what you think of me."

"Do you really?" he whispered back as he sank down beside her on the edge of the bed, releasing her neck only to grasp her chin roughly. "You little idiot! What do you know about men? How could you possibly know what I think?"

"How could I possibly *not* know?" she retorted, flexing her shoulders, wishing he would loosen his tight grip on her. "I'm not stupid, Adam; I've told you that before. I *see* how you act; I *sense* all the aggravation you feel. And that tells me pretty clearly what you think of me."

An expression that seemed almost to convey regret played across his lean features, but only for an instant. Then it was gone.

"Susan, you're wrong," he stated flatly, his eyes dark and unreadable. "Completely wrong."

"I am not! I know when you look at me all you see is a nuisance."

"I see nothing of the sort," he said wearily. "I can assure you a nuisance is not at all how I would describe you."

"Isn't it?" she exclaimed recklessly, some feminine instinct awakening in her that compelled her to jolt him from his indifference. Without stopping to consider what a dangerous game she was initiating, she slipped her bedjacket off, exposing the satiny skin of her shoulders and her slender, shapely arms. "Look at me. How would you describe me, then, if not as a nuisance? Do you think I'm pretty enough now, or sophisticated? Of course you don't. You didn't even notice I have this gown on, much less think I look alluring in it. So how *would* you describe me if I'm not pretty or sophisticated or intelligent or sexy?"

"You're playing with fire, little girl," he muttered through clenched teeth as his narrowed eyes traveled over the length of her body. Then, when he suddenly reached out to push the gown's straps off her shoulders and she took a sharp, startled breath, he smiled mockingly. "What's the matter? Isn't that the kind of reaction you thought you wanted? Too bad if it isn't. It's too late to change your mind now. You're going to find out exactly how seeing you in that gown affected me."

Almost of their own volition, her fingers tangled in the thick hair at the nape of his neck as his hands spanned her slim waist. And that involuntary response was more than Adam could withstand. What had begun as a warning suddenly became the danger itself. His arms slid roughly around her, crushing her slight body against the hard strength of his.

"*Adam!*" she whispered eagerly, wrapping her arms around his neck as he lowered her down on the bed. She gazed up at him, nearly hypnotized by the passion that glimmered in his eyes, moaning softly as his mouth descended with rough demand on her own. And as his lean, muscular body pressed her down into the softness of the mattress, she realized wonderingly that no man had ever been so close to her or been allowed to touch her so intimately. Yet she felt no fear, only an unfamiliar weakening of her limbs as his hands moved with gentle persuasion over her breasts to her waist to the tantalizing upward curve of her hips, warming her skin through the thin satin.

As his teeth closed gently on her earlobe, she slipped her hands inside his shirt, smiling with sensual satisfaction as he groaned. And when his mouth took hers again, slowly, with deepening deliberation, she knew instinctively that he might not want to stop this time. But maybe she didn't want him to stop anyway. It seemed so right for him to be here with her, needing her as she had needed him for so long. She loved him.

When his hand slipped inside the bodice of her gown to cover her breast, she was unable to protest.

"You're so warm," he murmured huskily as he pressed hot, urgent kisses along her throat. "Do you have any idea what you're doing to me, letting me touch you this way? Do you think I'm going to be able to let you go?"

"Aren't you?" she whispered against his ear, unaware of the uncertain quaver in her voice.

But obviously Adam detected it because he raised himself up slightly to look down into her eyes.

"You're scared," he stated softly. "Aren't you?"

"No," she answered automatically, then admitted: "Well, maybe a little nervous."

"Would you be if we were someplace alone? Would you be if we were at my house?"

"I-I don't know, I-I . . ."

"Will you spend a weekend there with me?" he asked, his dark eyes searching her face. "Soon, very soon? When you're feeling completely well again? We could make some excuse to Uncle Josh about being away at the same time. You could tell him you're going home for a brief visit. Or we could even tell him the truth, that we're spending the weekend together. Would you do that?"

Never before had she felt so torn by indecision. With his hands still gently caressing her waist, every nerve in her body seemed to be urging her to say yes, but the values that had been instilled in her through the years overruled the physical needs he aroused. She could not say yes, no matter how much she wanted to. If he became her lover someday in a moment of uncontrollable passion, she might never regret her surrender. But to plan such an event would cheapen it somehow and she knew she might always despise herself for letting it become less special than she had always imagined it would be. With a tremulous sigh and a genuinely regretful look in her dark violet eyes, she shook her head.

"I-I'm sorry but I just couldn't," she whispered haltingly. "To just plan it w-would . . ."

Uttering an incomprehensible exclamation, he rolled away from her, to sit up on the edge of the bed, raking his fingers through his hair.

"This has to stop," he muttered abruptly, not bothering to even look at her. "It's obvious we see sexual relationships in entirely different lights, and I see no evidence that that's going to change. So, do me a favor, will you? If I'm ever fool enough to let something like this begin again, tell me no at the beginning. You'll be saving me a hell of a lot of frustration."

Sitting up, Susan laid her hand imploringly on his arm, then flinched as he shook it off immediately. And as he strode to the door without a backward glance and went out, closing it behind him with more force than was necessary, she could only stare after him, her eyes dark with pain.

She should be counting herself lucky, she tried to tell herself. If he wanted nothing more from her than her warm body, it was good that she realized she was not willing to be used. Let him find some girl who took intimacy as lightly as he did. She herself would survive if he never so much as touched her again; she had for twenty-one years before she met him. Yet, as she lay down and turned her face into the pillow, such logic failed to comfort her in the least.

Chapter Ten

By the first Monday in November, Susan was feeling nearly normal again after two weeks of gradually rebuilding her strength. Though she still seemed to tire easily, she attributed that as much to emotional lethargy as to a slow recovery. Even the tense, tenuous relationship she and Adam had shared before that night in her bedroom had disintegrated now, until she felt as if they were strangers. Whenever possible he avoided her, and if he had to be near her she was overwhelmingly aware of the cool, distant manner with which he treated her.

She was depressed. Even Joshua's rising excitement about the ball could not elicit her enthusiasm. Now, five days before the big event, she simply went about her business solemnly.

The arrangements were complete, for the most part. She and Emily had decided on the refreshments to be served and she had contacted the caterers. Adam had hired men to move some of the excess furniture out of the huge drawing room across the hall from the library, and the remaining sofas and chairs had been arranged along the walls to make room for dancing. Now that room and all the rest of the house gleamed after Emily had spent more than a week polishing and cleaning. The silver shone, the crystal sparkled, and every wood surface in the house had been buffed to mirror brightness. Even Baker had been busy on the grounds until the outside of the house looked as elegant and orderly as the interior.

Every day, Susan and Joshua revised the list they were keeping of those people who accepted invitations. And as it grew longer with each passing day, she began to see that very few of the invited had declined.

"It looks like the whole county's going to be here Saturday night," she remarked Monday afternoon. "Do you think we'll have enough room for all of them?"

"We never had any problem making room for all of them before. The overflow always used to spill out into the hall, but it didn't matter since there's room for dancing out there too." Joshua grinned wryly. "Besides, some of the men spend most of the evening gathered around the punch bowl in the dining room."

"Well, let's just hope nobody ruins their fun by dropping a wig in the liquid refreshment this year," she said, smiling as he laughed. "I'd hate for anyone not to have a good time."

Joshua tilted his head to one side, eyeing her questioningly. "And what about you? Do you think you're going to have a good time?"

"Sure, why shouldn't I?" she murmured, bending her head so he could not see the truth in her face. "I'm looking forward to the ball. I've never been to one, you know."

"And what have you decided to wear? What lovely young lady from history are you going to come as?"

"I really don't know yet," she told him, sweeping a strand of dark hair back behind her ear. "I thought I'd go into Atlanta tomorrow or Wednesday and see what I can find at the costume shop. I'm sure they'll have something that'll do."

"Oh, but don't you want something special?" he persisted. "Remember, now, this is a costume ball, not a masquerade, so you won't have a mask to hide behind if you're feeling a little shy. Everybody will know you—they just might not know who you're supposed to be."

She lifted her hand in a gesture that almost seemed indifferent. "I'm sure I'll find something suitable. Any old thing will do, I guess."

"Any old thing most certainly will *not* do!" Joshua protested, shaking his finger chidingly at her. "You should be the belle of the ball—and with the surprise I have for you, I imagine you will be." Smiling mysteriously, he stood. "Close your eyes now while I go get Emily to bring it down."

Obeying, she sat back against the sofa cushions, feeling rather like a fool squeezing her eyelids tightly shut, but that's what he had wanted so she did not cheat by opening them. After a few long minutes, she heard movement out in the hall.

"Okay, you can look now," Joshua announced abruptly.

When Susan turned toward the doorway, she could hardly believe what she saw Emily holding up with a proud grin.

It was Felicity's dress—or at least it looked exactly like the one she had worn when she had sat for the portrait that hung above a table in the hall. A midnight-blue silk, its skirt had three wide lace-edged flounces, and the tight-fitting bodice was cut low to expose a provocative hint of cleavage, baring the shoulders to the tiny puffed sleeves.

Susan's surprised eyes darted to Joshua, who was smiling and nodding his head encouragingly.

"Recognize it?" he asked excitedly. "It's an exact copy."

"It's magnificent," Susan assured him, getting up to walk across the room to take a better look. "Oh, Emily, did you make this yourself? If you did, you're a fabulous seamstress."

The housekeeper's cheeks colored slightly at the

praise. "My sister helped me," she explained. "Took us near three weeks to get it done, even working together. But I think it turned out nice." Then, as Susan lifted out the sides of the full skirt, she added: "You'll have to wear a hoop to show it off just right."

"You mean it really is for me?" Susan asked incredulously, unable to take her eyes off the dress. "You really want me to wear this Saturday night?"

"Well, *I'm* not about to wear it," Joshua quipped, then laughed merrily. "Of course it's for you. Don't you like it?"

"Oh, yes, I love it," she told him hastily, giving him an impulsive hug that pleased him very much. "I just hope I'll look as nice in it as Felicity does in that portrait. I may not, you know. She was blond, and with my dark hair—"

"You'll look beautiful," he interrupted emphatically. "She had nice dark blue eyes, but they couldn't have been as lovely as yours, and this dress should really show off their violet color perfectly."

"I-I really don't know what to say," Susan whispered as she examined the exquisite detailing of the dress. "It's so sweet of you to want me to wear it, and you did such a beautiful job, Emily. Thank you both."

As the housekeeper beamed with pride, Joshua gave Susan an indulgent, affectionate smile. "I thought you'd enjoy wearing it, since I've seen you looking at that portrait in the hall so often."

Nodding, Susan pretended to be very interested in the fine lace that edged the flounces of the dress. What Joshua did not realize was that she had spent so much time staring at the portrait because in it Jonathan Thornton stood behind his seated wife, resting a lean brown hand on her bare shoulder. It was the disturbing resemblance to Adam, which she saw in the strong, sensual shape of his mouth and in his dark, intelligent eyes, that fascinated her. But that was her secret, she thought with some relief until Joshua's next words made her wonder nervously if perhaps he was much more perceptive than she had believed.

"Adam's agreed to come as Jonathan, by the way," he said idly, apparently unaware of the sharp, swift breath she took. "And since you'll be in this dress, I thought you two might serve as host and hostess for me. Would you mind?"

For a moment Susan only looked at him, reluctant to refuse since he had been kind enough to go to the trouble and expense of having the dress made for her. Finally she nodded.

"It's all right with me," she said dully. "But I'm not so sure Adam will go for the idea. He'd probably rather not be stuck with me all evening," she muttered. "He'd probably rather invite one of the girls he goes out with occasionally."

"He hasn't mentioned wanting to invite anybody to me," said Joshua with a puzzled frown. "And he didn't object to the idea of being with you."

"You mean he knows you want us to host this ball? Together?" she exclaimed. "And he knows I'm supposed to be Felicity?" When Joshua nodded rather bewilderedly, she had to bite back a dismayed groan. Now she understood why Adam had been in such an oddly pensive mood recently. Protective as he was of his precious bachelorhood, he must be hating the very idea of pretending to be Jonathan while she, of all people, would be playing the role of Felicity.

Susan was dressed early for the ball Saturday night— and that, she realized immediately, was a mistake. As she paced back and forth before the mirror, pausing occasionally to unnecessarily smooth the shining sweeps of dark hair that were pulled back from her face into a loose chignon on the nape of her neck, she had too much time to think. What would Adam think of her in this dress? Surely, despite all their differences, he would have to admit, at least to himself, that she looked pretty. Even she, self-critical as she was, could see that the dress complimented her figure and her coloring and did indeed accent her wide violet eyes as Joshua had promised it would. The bodice, however, was cut much lower than she had realized before trying it on for the first time, and she had never before worn anything, not even a suimsuit, that exposed so much of the generous curve of her breasts. How odd it was that women in Felicity's day could not expose their ankles but could wear low-cut gowns that barely covered their bosoms. It was an inconsistency she had never understood and she still did not. But who cared about such trivialities now.

She dreaded the evening. Since that night in her bedroom, Adam had been so different, so much more quiet than he had been before. Sometimes, in the evenings, when they sat in the library with Joshua, she would look up to find him watching her, his expression a mystery she was afraid to try to analyze. Besides, she was nearly certain what he must be thinking. He had never trusted her and had identified her with Felicity and himself with Jonathan, imagining, she supposed, that he might be lured into the same kind of relationship they had shared and subsequently into a necessary marriage. It had never occurred to him that Jonathan had eventually found great happiness with Felicity and might even really have loved her all along and simply been too stubborn to admit it. But that thought would never occur to him, because he was not in love.

Sighing again, she glanced at the clock on the night table and saw that it was seven thirty, not too early to go downstairs. After freshening her lipstick, she went to peek out her door and saw that Adam's was standing ajar. Obviously he had already gone downstairs, and, after taking a deep, shaky breath, she went down too.

Both Adam and Joshua were in the library having a drink, talking quietly together, and she hovered outside the doorway, suddenly too shy to call attention to herself. To do so would have been unnecessary anyway since Joshua looked up after a few seconds, beaming a smile when he found her standing there. But his friendly welcome was soon pushed completely from her mind when Adam turned, then slowly stood, his eyes never leaving her.

He looked magnificent and so much like Jonathan that it almost seemed as if the portrait in the hall had come alive. Close-fitting black trousers emphasized the muscular lines of his long legs while the flaring black coat was made less severe by the pleated white shirt he wore beneath it. And the intricate black cravat at his throat accentuated the silvery-blond hair. But it was the darkening intensity of those green eyes that made her suddenly aware that she was being inspected also. As a warming blush colored her cheeks, he came to her, taking her hand and tucking it into the crook of his elbow as he escorted her into the room.

"Perfect," Joshua Thornton said as he examined the two of them. "My old neighbors are sure going to get a kick out of being welcomed to Maiden's Bower by Jonathan and Felicity themselves."

Glancing up warily at Adam, Susan was astonished to see the indulgent smile he gave his uncle. She had expected indifference if not actual hostility but saw no indication that he was feeling either. Now, if he would only remain in this benevolent mood, the evening would be considerably easier for her to get through.

Receiving the guests started out rather uncomfortably, however, when a few of the older and more outspoken neighbors made teasing remarks about the scandalous beginning of Jonathan's marriage to Felicity. But when she realized Adam was only grinning good-naturedly at their kidding insinuations, she began to relax and managed to maintain her composure even with the arrival of some of Adam's friends, including the rather birdbrained Monica, who chattered incessantly until her Teddy dragged her away. Greeting

Nellie Brooks did shake her composure to some extent, however, especially when the woman surveyed her dress, particularly the low-cut bodice, with a grimace of disdain. Then she and the mild-mannered, soft-spoken young man she had in tow ambled off toward the drawing room and Adam and Susan were left alone in the large hall, except for Baker, who was serving as doorman for the moment.

"Except for a few stragglers, I imagine that's the lot of them," Adam said, holding out his arm for her to take, then escorting her into the mingling crowd in the drawing room.

For a few moments they simply moved from group to group, engaging in idle chitchat. While Adam did most of the talking, Susan looked around the large room with satisfaction. Joshua had left it to her to decide how it should be decorated and she had kept it quite simple. A few small potted trees and exotic plants were complimented by the dried-bouquets of yellow marigolds, orange zinnias, maidenhair ferns, and short shafts of wheat that were arranged strategically in small earthenware vases on the small tables and in tall wicker baskets that sat on the floor.

After a few minutes of roaming through the crowd, Joshua approached them, saying it was time for the dancing to begin. As the musicians started playing a lively waltz, the crowd drew back along the walls, waiting. Susan swallowed with difficulty, trying to ease her sudden nervousness. She had dreaded this moment for days. Never having danced in a hoop skirt before, she had no desire to make a spectacle of herself as she and Adam led the first dance. He would not relish that, she was certain, but it was his duty as host and hers as hostess to see it through.

Happily, he hid his reluctance behind a smile as he escorted her to the center of the polished wood floor, then slid his arm securely around her waist. And after only a few seconds into the dance she breathed a sigh of relief, finding his lead amazingly easy to follow as they glided around the room. Then other couples joined them on the floor and she no longer had to feel like the center of attention.

When he drew her closer against him as the dance floor became more crowded, she smiled hesitantly up at him, realizing for the first time how tall he was. Now the top of her head only reached the pocket of his black coat, but that was because she was wearing low-heeled satin slippers like the ones that peeked out from beneath Felicity's dress in the portrait.

"The ball seems to be a success," he said, his warm breath caressing her ear. "Look at Uncle Josh over there. He's having a great time."

After Susan glanced over her shoulder at his uncle, she smiled back up at him. "Planning everything has made him so happy," she said softly. "I'm glad you thought of having a ball this year."

"And I'm glad you were willing to help us prepare for it," he answered, a warmth in his tone she had not heard for days. Then he held her away from him slightly as his gaze moved slowly down the length of her body. "Did I tell you I think you look especially beautiful in that dress?" When her eyes widened and she shook her head, he said teasingly, "Well, consider yourself told now—because you do."

Lowering her eyes, she murmured her thanks and stared at the strong tanned column of his neck above the black silk cravat, wishing he did not have the power to play havoc with her emotions. She tried to convince herself that the compliment had come from a desire to be polite, nothing more, and she should have sense enough to accept it as such. But it was impossible to remember that as he added softly:

"You know, sometimes I get the strange feeling you're going to be a part of my life for a long time to come, no matter what I do. Do you ever get that feeling about people?"

As her startled eyes searched his face, she could not gather her wits about her sufficiently to even nod in response.

"Well?" he persisted, giving her an inexpressibly tender smile. "Do you, Susan?"

"S-sometimes I d-do," she stammered finally, unable to look away. "I-I . . ."

"Do you have that feeling about me?"

"I-I did, but then . . . well, yes, sometimes I still do."

"I wonder what it means," he whispered musingly, brushing his lips against her forehead as he gathered her closer to the warm strength of his body. "Don't you wonder too?"

Completely confused yet oddly happy, she could only nod as she closed her eyes and pressed her cheek against his chest. And when the dance ended and he led her toward a sofa at the end of the room, she felt the loss of his arms around her keenly. Yet the smile he gave her as they sat down on the sofa went a long way toward dispelling that sense of loss.

"You do look lovely," he said abruptly, a certain exciting urgency in his tone. And he gazed at her parted lips with such intensity that she felt as if he had actually kissed her. But then he released the hand he held in both of his. "Don't run away," he commanded gently. "I'll go get you a cup of punch. Or would you rather join me and have something stronger?"

"Anything," she whispered bemusedly, hardly able to believe the change in him. After watching him stride away toward the dining room, she sank back on the sofa, pressing her fingers against her lips. He could be the most magnetic man when he was not constantly putting her on the defensive, and at that moment she would have done anything to make sure they would always be a part of each other's lives. Closing her eyes, she let the warm contentment she was feeling sweep over her, but unfortunately that sense of well-being was short-lived.

"Well, aren't you looking smug?" a catty voice interrupted her reverie. "If I were you, I'd try not to look so much like the cat that swallowed the canary."

Susan opened her eyes warily as Nellie Brooks invited herself to sit down. Sorry as she was to see the woman, she did try to act pleasant.

"Hello, Miss Brooks. Having a nice time?"

"Oh, so-so, I suppose," Nellie drawled, twirling a black strand of the Cleopatra wig she wore. "But I guess I just don't see much sense in dwelling in the past, so parties like this don't thrill me very much."

Then go, Susan thought uncharitably, but she forced a slight smile. "I'm just the opposite," she commented civilly. "I think it's a lot of fun to dress up and pretend to be somebody from long ago."

"Yes, I imagine you would," Nellie snapped at her, her eyes flashing. "Look who you chose to come as." She smirked. "Don't you think you're being a little obvious, dear?"

"Obvious?"

"Oh, don't play the innocent with me. I'm not Adam, who's apparently taken in by your sugary sweetness. You know exactly what I mean by obvious. It's certainly plain enough that you hope Adam will decide to marry you the way Jonathan Thornton married that Florence or Freda or whatever her name was."

"You're very much mistaken," Susan said stiffly, clenching her fingers around the fan she held in her hand. "I'm well aware of Adam's philosophy concerning marriage, and I'm certainly not stupid enough to believe he's going to change the way he feels because of me. And, by the way, her name was Felicity."

Nellie waved that last comment away with a disparaging flick of her wrist. "Come on now," she said sarcastically. "I told you you don't have to keep up that act with me. What besides marriage would you be wanting enough to spend the night with Adam? It's not a job as I thought, or you would have gone in for that interview with Kay Mead."

"How do you know anything about Kay Mead?" Susan exclaimed, sitting up straighter, her muscles tensing. "How do you know she called me about an interview?"

"I asked her to call you, that's how," Nellie said with infuriating calm as she examined her long, sharp fingernails. "Kay and I went to school together."

"So it was you. I wondered who had given her my number out here."

The older woman gave her an unpleasant, self-satisfied smile. "Of course, Adam asked me to do it. He felt sure you'd take the job if Kay eventually offered it. And she might have since you do have some reporting experience, if you can call what you did for that dinky little newspaper reporting."

"Are you trying to tell me Adam hoped I would take that job?" Susan asked incredulously. Of course that possibility had occurred to her, but right now Nellie seemed too eager to convince her it was true. On impulse, she issued a challenge. "I don't believe Adam would want that, if for no other reason than he wouldn't want his uncle to be upset, which he would be if I left before his family history is finished."

"Oh, don't be such a idiot," Nellie said disgustedly. "I won't deny he cares for his uncle, but you're such an aggravation to him that he decided to try to lure you away from here."

Only two hours ago Susan would have found this story plausible, but now, after what Adam had said tonight and the way he had acted toward her, she doubted very much that Nellie was telling the truth. And she lost no more time saying she didn't believe it.

Nellie sniffed. "Believe what you want, but one thing's for certain. Adam's getting extremely tired of putting up with you. Men get bored so quickly, you know, even when girls will spend nights with them."

Susan's lips pressed tightly together. Enough was enough, and she longed to slap the older girl's smug face.

"You know darn well I didn't spend the night at Adam's for the reason you've been telling everyone!"

"But you'd like to spend the night with him for that reason, wouldn't you?" Nellie retorted. "If you could get him involved that way, you'd at least have some chance of trapping him into marriage."

"Oh, go away, Nellie," Susan said before she could stop herself. But she really did not regret saying it, especially when the woman shrugged, then got up to go on her way. "Witch," she muttered, watching her go. But after a moment some of her anger dissolved and all the doubts she had ever had concerning Adam's feelings came back to her in an overwhelming rush. What if Nellie had actually been telling the truth? What if he really was so anxious to be rid of her he would risk upsetting his uncle? What if . . . There were so many what ifs and his attitude toward her had been so confusing in the past that the affection he had seemed to be showing her tonight was not enough to make her feel very secure.

There was only one way to find out the real truth, though, and that was to ask Adam himself. As she watched him coming toward her, carrying two drinks, she resolved to do just that. But when she took the cup of punch he'd brought, she discovered her hands were shaking violently.

"What's wrong?" he asked worriedly when he saw how she was trembling. "Aren't you feeling well?"

"I'm all right," she told him with a nervous little smile, trying to steel herself for what might be about to come. "It's just that I've had another little run-in with Nellie Brooks. And she told me something that I don't know whether to believe or not."

"Well, I'd advise you to take anything she says with a grain of salt," he stated wryly. "After all, you're not her favorite person and she wouldn't be above telling a lie if she thought it would upset you."

"You could tell me if it's true or not," she said softly, watching him with wide, apprehensive eyes. "What she told me was about you."

"You're really upset, aren't you?" he asked with sudden seriousness, reaching out to caress her cheek with the back of his hand. "Tell me what she said."

"Did you ask her to get her friend Kay Mead to offer me a job on her newspaper?" she asked, her words rushed.

"I haven't asked Nellie to do anything," he answered with a puzzled frown. "And I don't even know a Kay Mead. Why? What's all this about?"

"You really don't know, do you?" she whispered, her eyes shining happily. "Somehow I knew you didn't."

"Well, would you mind telling me what you're talking about?" After she explained fully, he shook his head in mock admonition. "You mean at first you really suspected I might have had her call? Susan, don't you know me a little better than that? I told you when you first came here that I meant for you to stay until Uncle Josh had finished his history."

"I thought maybe you'd changed your mind," she said quietly. "I thought you might want to get rid of me since I seem to bother you so much."

"Oh, you bother me all right," he murmured, his eyes narrowing as they surveyed her face. "But not the way you just meant." Then, as she gazed up at him, he touched her chin with gentle fingers and lowered his head to kiss her lightly. His mouth lingered against hers for an instant before he pulled away. "I never thought

I'd say this," he murmured rather huskily, "but I'm beginning to see why Jonathan got himself involved with Felicity."

"Are you?" she whispered breathlessly. "Tell me why."

"Later," he whispered back, his eyes full of promise. "We'll talk later, after all these people are gone." And with a smile that he had never bestowed on her before, he led her back onto the dance floor.

Unfortunately, they did not get that chance to talk when all the people had gone, because as the last of the guests were going out the door Joshua was suddenly stricken with severe chest pains.

After alerting Dr. Jennings, Adam and Susan rushed him to the hospital, where he was whisked away on a stretcher. After watching him being taken away with a horrible feeling of helplessness, she went with Adam into the small room where they had waited once before.

"He was so pale," she murmured, almost to herself. Then she clutched Adam's sleeve. "Do you . . . do you think it's his . . . his . . . "

"His heart?" Adam nodded, closing his eyes with an unhappy sigh. "I think it must be."

Something vulnerable in his expression made her ache to comfort him. Slipping her hand into his, she pressed closer against his side.

"He was conscious," she said consolingly. "That's got to be a good sign."

"I hope so!" he exclaimed softly, squeezing her small fingers tightly. "Why tonight? He was enjoying himself so much."

Not knowing what to say, Susan did not attempt an answer. All she could do was cling to his hand and hope for the best.

For the next two hours they said very little and the time dragged by with maddening slowness. Since their arrival with Joshua, no one had told them anything.

Finally Adam could stand the suspense no longer. As he stood to go out and see what was happening, Dr. Jennings strode into the waiting room. He waved them back into their seats.

"He's spunky, I'll say that for him," the doctor began, perching himself on a low table in front of the sofa where they sat. "And stronger than I thought. He's had a mild heart seizure, Adam, but if we can keep him quiet so he doesn't bring on another one, he should be all right."

Adam expelled his breath in a rush of relief. "Do you think all the excitement about the ball is what caused it?"

Dr. Jennings shrugged. "Could have, I suppose. Or it could have happened anyway. It's hard to say. One thing's for certain this time, though," he added emphatically. "He's not going to talk himself out of this hospital before I think he's ready to go. He's going to have to put that history right out of his mind for a few weeks. It excites him too much, and we're just going to have to make him understand it's going to have to wait."

"Any ideas on how to accomplish that?" Adam asked with a wry grin. "You know how stubborn he can be."

"How could I not know that? I've been his doctor for fifteen years. But we're still going to have to make him see he can't even talk about it for a while. He just gets too involved in it." Dr. Jennings stood. "We'll convince him somehow, don't worry. Now, if you want to see him for a minute before you go, you'll have to wait until they've gotten him settled in CCU—cardiac care unit. I'll have a nurse tell you when you can go up. But don't stay long."

Assuring him that they wouldn't, Adam watched the doctor rush away, then turned back to Susan, a relieved smile on his face.

But she was not able to smile because a terrible thought had just occurred to her.

"Maybe I should go home—to Forest Falls, I mean—until he has a chance to get better," she suggested abruptly, unenthusiastically, as she looked up at Adam. "I'm afraid if I'm around he might not be able to stop thinking about that history. If I go home, though, until he's better, he'll have to put it out of his mind."

"No. No, you can't go," Adam said firmly as he sat back down beside her. "He'd be upset if you went away, and that wouldn't do him any good. You have to stay, Susan."

"Just for his sake?" she questioned breathlessly. "Is that why I have to stay?"

As his gaze held hers, he shook his head slowly.

"I want you to stay for my sake too," he admitted, drawing her close against him. "I think we could have something very special together, Susan, and I want you here with me so we can find out for sure. Will you stay for that reason?"

"Oh, yes, *yes*," she whispered, sliding her arms around his waist. "Yes, I'll—"

"Adam, darling," Nellie Brooks interrupted shrilly from the doorway, then bustled into the room. "I heard about poor Mr. Thornton, and since I go right by here on my way home I had to stop to see how he is."

"Why don't I go get us some coffee?" Susan suggested softly as she moved away from Adam. "You can talk to Nellie while I'm gone."

Though smiling regretfully, he nodded his agreement, then handed her some loose change to pay for the coffee before turning his attention to his associate.

Walking down the hall toward the vending machines, Susan hardly noticed the curious stares her ball dress received. She was too happy in that moment to even realize that other people besides Adam existed. "Something very special together," he had said. Her imagination took off on wild meanderings as she slid a quarter into the coin slot and watched the cup fill. And, as she walked back toward the waiting room, she was smiling secretively until she heard Nellie talking more loudly than she should have been in a hospital. Hearing her own name, she stopped to listen.

"I just don't understand what you see in her," Nellie was saying with a great deal of impatience. "I mean, she's been nothing but trouble to you from the start."

"I caused most of the trouble myself," Adam answered calmly. "Most of the problems were not Susan's fault."

"But she is so—"

"I really don't see that this is any of your business, Nellie," he interrupted stiffly. "I don't need your advice."

"But I'm just trying to keep you from making a big mistake, Adam! You don't want to get yourself involved with this girl. She's such a child. What can you possibly have in common with her? Your friends will probably never accept her. She simply won't fit in."

"Oh, for heaven's sake, Nellie, don't you think I know that?" he suddenly exclaimed, something like resentment in his harsh tone. "You're not telling me a thing I don't already know. But maybe . . ."

Unwilling to hear the rest, Susan rushed away, back down the hall, her throat constricting painfully with tears she could not allow herself to give in to in such a public place. What a simpleton she was, she thought bitterly. What Adam had meant by something special together had obviously not been what she had hoped he meant. To her something special meant a permanent commitment. Anything less would not really be special at all. But he was a sophisticate and to him special probably meant a brief, tempestuous affair that eventually ended without regrets from either person involved, and that was what he wanted from her. That was all he

could want, if he was so sure she would never really fit
into the kind of life he led. An affair could never be
enough for her, though, not loving him the way she did.
But if she stayed here near him, it might be impossible
to resist seeking even that little bit of happiness. And
that meant she did not dare stay.

Chapter Eleven

After dinner Monday evening Susan excused herself and went straight up to her room, but she hardly had time to do more than stretch out on her bed before her mother followed.

"You didn't really say how long you'd be home, honey," Helen Thomas commented as she picked up her daughter's suitcase to move it out of the way. Then, with a frown, she put it back down. "Why, you haven't even unpacked yet. Aren't you afraid everything will get wrinkled?"

"I'll do it in a few minutes," Susan murmured, turning over onto her back but still not opening her eyes. "I just wanted to rest awhile."

Mrs. Thomas sat down on the edge of the bed. "Are you sure you're over that bout of pneumonia?" she asked worriedly. "You've been dragging around the house since you got here this afternoon."

"I'm just tired."

"Are you sure there isn't something else wrong?" her mother persisted gently. "I think there is because you give me such vague answers when I ask you questions and ever since you were a little girl you always did that whenever something was bothering you. Why don't you tell me what it is? Coming home to wait for Mr. Thornton to get better shouldn't be making you this unhappy."

"I am worried about him, Mama," Susan said defensively, not wanting to be questioned yet. "He *is* in the hospital."

"Yes, but you said he seemed to be feeling better when you went by there this morning before catching the bus," Mrs. Thomas argued. "And I still think something else has upset you. It wouldn't have anything to do with Mr. Thornton's nephew, would it?"

Susan heaved a resigned sigh. "Why can't I ever hide anything from you?" she muttered dully. "I don't know how you knew it had something to do with him, since I haven't even mentioned his name since I got home."

"You're my little girl," her mother said with some amusement. "I always know when something's going on in your life. And I could tell by your voice when you called me on the phone that this Adam Kincaid was important to you."

Important. That certainly was an understatement, Susan thought ruefully, squeezing her eyelids tightly closed, trying not to cry. Somehow Adam had become much more than important. Now he was essential and she did not know how she was ever going to stop wanting him, much less forget him altogether, especially if she kept her promise to Joshua and went back to Maiden's Bower in a month or so when he was better so they could complete his history. When she had made that promise, a month seemed a long enough time to enable her to get over Adam to some extent; but, judging by the way she felt right now, eternity would not be long enough. And she dreaded the thought of having to go back there in a few weeks still as much in love with him as she was now.

"Ah, well," she finally forced herself to say cheerily as she opened her eyes and propped herself up on her elbows. "He may be important to me, but I'm afraid the feeling isn't mutual."

"Why? Has he got a girlfriend?"

"Oodles of them, I imagine."

"But no one special?"

Susan's answering laugh nearly caught on a sob but she suppressed it just in time. "Adam doesn't believe in special relationships, at least the kind you mean, Mama."

"And that's why you're unhappy?"

"No. I'm unhappy because I was dumb enough to fall in love with him, knowing he didn't believe in them," Susan retorted bitterly. "Aren't people always unhappy when they see what nitwits they've been?"

"Oh, honey, you're not a nitwit," her mother said urgently, reaching out to brush a wayward strand of hair from Susan's cheek. "Falling in love is nothing to be ashamed of."

Susan sniffed disbelievingly. "Why do I feel ashamed, then? And so much like a fool?"

"I don't know why," Helen Thomas murmured, eyeing her daughter suspiciously. "Are you sure he doesn't care about you? Surely he must have given you some kind of encouragement for you to fall in love with him?"

"I guess I just wanted him to care about me so much, I made more of the things he said and did than I should have."

"Well, what did he say when you told him you were coming home for a few weeks? Did he act as if he cared?"

"I didn't tell him," Susan muttered, watching her fingers as they plucked at the white chenille bedspread. "I don't imagine it'll matter all that much to him, though." Suddenly, she sighed wearily. "Look, could we talk about something else?"

"Sure," her mother said softly, sympathetically. Then she stood. "I do wish you'd come with Terry and me to Macon for the night. While he sees his customers tomorrow, you could spend the day with me at Aunt Lily's."

Though Susan smiled gratefully, she still shook her

head. "No, thanks. I just don't feel up to sitting over there and having to yell everything I say right into her ear because she's too stubborn to get a hearing aid. And please don't worry about me being here by myself tonight. I'll be just fine and I won't get lonely. I plan to go to bed very early."

Nodding, her mother leaned down to kiss her cheek. "Try not to be so unhappy," she said kindly. "These things usually have a way of working out right in the end."

But this *was* the end, wasn't it? And things certainly had not worked out, Susan thought as her mother left the room. Yet she really shouldn't be all that surprised that they hadn't. All along her common sense had tried to tell her that Adam could never be serious about her. It was just that her emotions had not cooperated and now she was paying for her foolishness. She only hoped she could get over the worst of the pain before she had to keep her promise to Joshua and go back to Maiden's Bower.

Two hours later, after a long cry and a hot bath to wash the tears away, Susan wrapped herself in her floor-length terry robe, then padded out into her room. It was chilly, especially with the sound of a brisk wind rattling the branches of the dogwood tree outside her window. Rubbing her arms, she curled up on the easy chair beside her bed, trying to think what she might do that would make her sleepy. Reading was out—she would never be able to concentrate—and she simply did not have the energy to go downstairs to see what was on television. So she did nothing for several minutes except stare blindly across the room, wondering what Adam was doing right now. Then the doorbell rang, interrupting her pensive thoughts.

"Now what!" she uttered disgustedly as she swung her feet to the floor. She was in no mood for company, especially if the visitor turned out to be Fern from next door, coming over to gossip on and on about the rest of the neighbors. Maybe if she didn't answer and was very, very still, whoever was there would give up and go away, she thought halfway down the stairs. But the next long ring was punctuated by several hard, loud knocks, so she gave up that foolish hope and hurried down the remaining steps. Stopping before the door, she lapped the lapels of the robe tighter across her breasts and retied the belt. Then she stood on tiptoe to peek out the door's small square window, but when she saw who was standing beneath the bright porch light she dropped back down on her heels with a gasp.

It was Adam. Suddenly, her legs felt rubbery, as if they might collapse beneath her at any moment, and she clung to the doorknob, unable to think coherently for a few seconds. Then simultaneously, the ringing and the knocking began anew, and she jerked the door open simply to stop the nerve-racking noise.

Adam said nothing. His jaw tight, his lips pressed firmly together, he simply stared at her while she stared back.

After only a moment, she could stand the silence no longer.

"C-come in," she said, her voice breaking revealingly as she stepped aside for him to enter. As he brushed her arm in passing, she shrank back closer to the wall behind her.

"Are you alone?" he asked gruffly as his eyes swept over her. "If you're not, go get dressed and we'll go out somewhere in the car. What I have to say to you is private."

"Nobody else is here," she murmured as she closed the door again. Turning back to face him, she gestured toward the living room. "We can t-talk in there."

Nodding, he indicated she should precede him.

"Let me take your coat first," she suggested weakly. When he removed the light corduroy jacket and handed it to her, she tried not to notice the familiar spicy fragrance of his aftershave that came with it.

"I imagine you're surprised to see me here," he commented expressionlessly after she sat on a chair and he took a seat on the sofa. Stretching his long legs out in front of him, he lit a cigarette, then relaxed back to glare at her. "I suppose you thought I'd just let you walk away?"

Perching on the edge of the chair, she folded the sides of her robe tightly across her knees as she nodded without looking up at him. "I guess I did think that," she murmured. "I didn't think you'd really care whether I left or not."

"And may I ask what gave you such an idiotic notion?"

She shrugged, unwilling to admit that what he had said to Nellie Saturday night had hurt her deeply. "I just didn't think you'd care. Does it matter why I didn't?"

"Of course it matters! I wouldn't be here right now if it didn't, would I?" After grinding out his cigarette in the ashtray on the table beside him, he leaned toward her, resting his elbows on his knees, allowing his hands to hang limply between them. "Talk to me!" he muttered roughly, his dark eyes searching her face. "Tell me what you told Joshua this morning that you made him promise not to tell me."

Susan's cheeks colored. "What did he say I said?"

"Nothing, except that you had to come home for a while. He kept his promise, Susan. He wouldn't tell me the reason you gave him. But you're going to tell me right now, aren't you?"

"No," she whispered. "I can't." Then she uttered a frightened little cry as he suddenly reached out to grasp her arm and jerk her out of the chair to her knees on the floor before him. "Adam, please, don't do . . ."

His hands tangled in the hair on the nape of her neck as his thumbs lifted her chin.

"Tell me why you had to come home, Susan," he commanded. "Tell me right now or I'll—"

"Or you'll what?" she exclaimed, twisting her head in an effort to free herself. But resistance was useless and after a moment she ceased struggling, her eyes filling with tears. "Adam, please, just leave me alone."

"But I can't leave you alone! I never have been able to and you know that."

"Why? Why can't you?" she whispered miserably. "You don't want anything from me that you couldn't get from any other girl."

"That's where you're wrong," he whispered back, slightly relaxing his grip on her. "You have something nobody else can give, at least to me."

"And what is that?" she asked disbelievingly. "What have I got that's so special?"

"The same thing Felicity gave to Jonathan," he answered simply. "Innocence and—"

"I'm not the only innocent running around loose, Adam!"

"Will you shut up and let me finish?" he muttered, going down on his knees in front of her, sliding his arm around her waist to draw her close against his muscular chest. "Now, as I started to say: Innocence and, more important, love."

"*Love!* Hah! You don't want my . . ." She halted abruptly, stopped by the strange eager look in his eyes, catching her breath at what it seemed to mean. "Oh, Adam," she whispered urgently. "If you don't tell me what you're thinking, I'll go crazy."

"You already are crazy if you don't know," he muttered against her throat as he gathered her closer. "You little idiot, I'm in love with you. And if you're in love with me too, I want to hear you say it. Now. Are you?"

"Yes," she breathed incredulously, winding her slender arms around his neck. "Yes, I love you! But I didn't think—"

"Obviously not," he interrupted wryly as he took her mouth with a gentleness that changed abruptly to a searing, searching passion as his hands explored the rounded curves of her body. And as her softness yielded to his compelling strength, he pushed aside the lapels of her robe and his lips sought the scented hollow between her breasts. "You don't have anything on under this, do you?" he muttered hoarsely. And when she shook her head and tried to press closer against him, he held her away. "You'd better go put on some clothes right now or your parents may get the surprise of their lives when they come home."

Blushing, Susan started to get up, but apparently something in her shy expression changed his mind. Taking both her hands in a gentle grip, he rubbed his thumbs across her palms.

"Never mind," he whispered with a loving, indulgent smile. "I'll behave."

"But I might not," she confessed. "I never seem to want to behave when I'm with you."

"Umm, that is good news," he murmured suggestively, pressing light kisses along her cheek to her mouth. "If you mean that, then we should have a very memorable honeymoon."

Pulling away slightly, she gazed up at him, scarcely able to believe she had heard him correctly.

"Honeymoon? You mean you really want to marry me? I thought you were too happy being a bachelor."

"I thought so too until you came along. Then . . ." Shrugging, he grinned mischievously. "It could have been worse. At least I'm not as stubborn as old Jonathan was. You're not going to have to go through what Felicity did."

"But being pregnant with your baby wouldn't be such a terrible fate," she whispered, smiling as his hands tightened roughly around her waist. "Of course I suppose it would be more proper if we were married."

"Then we better get married. *Fast.* Before you *do* follow in Felicity's footsteps after all." He kissed her gently, then stood, pulling her up with him, then down on his lap as he sat on the sofa again. "But before we say anything else, I want to know exactly what made you come home today. I think you should know I could have almost murdered you when I got to Maiden's Bower this evening and Baker told me you had left. Then, when he told me you had stopped to see Uncle Josh before you left, I went to see him, hoping he would know why you'd gone."

"He did know why, but I made him promise not to tell you."

"Well, he didn't. I could have killed him too." When she murmured an urgent apology, his arms tightened around her. "Why *did* you leave? Yesterday you seemed happy. A little quiet, but happy."

"I can be a good actress for short periods of time."

"But what reason did you have to put on an act? Did I do something wrong? I thought we'd reached some sort of understanding Saturday night, even though I didn't get a chance to say all I wanted to."

Susan lowered her head, all the doubts nagging at her again.

"I heard what you said to Nellie at the hospital," she mumbled. "When she said I wouldn't fit in with your friends, you agreed with her."

His hand cupping her chin lifted her head back up.

"You mean to tell me you left because of that?" he exclaimed, shaking his head rather impatiently. "Didn't you hear what else I said to her?"

"That was enough."

"No, it was not enough. You missed the most important part. I did agree with Nellie that you won't fit in with my friends, and I still agree with that. *But* I told her and I'm telling you right now that that's one of the reasons I love you. You're a real person, Susan, and most of them don't know how to be real. I've discovered I don't want to fit in with them myself any longer. I'd rather be with you. You know what you want."

"I sure do," she whispered against his throat,

sliding her arms around his waist. "I want you; that's all."

"But you can have a career as a reporter too, if you'd still like to, after Uncle Josh's history is done. You would probably make a very good copywriter at the agency too, since you have such a creative imagination. Or you could even stay home and have babies. Whatever you decide's all right with me as long as we stay together. And speaking of together, I hope you won't make me wait long to marry you while you get ready for a big formal wedding. You won't, will you?"

"Would until this Saturday be too long to wait?"

"I guess I can stand it," he answered wryly, touching his lips to the parted softness of hers, gathering her closer as her hands caressed his back. "Autumn's ending, Susan, and it's getting cold outside," he said softly against her mouth. "Would you consider going home with me tonight to start keeping me warm for the winter?"

"Is that a proposition?"

"If it were, would you accept it?"

"This time, under the circumstances," she replied between light, teasing kisses, "I think I will. And we won't even have to go back to Atlanta. My parents won't be coming home tonight so we can stay right here."

"In separate bedrooms?" he asked hoarsely. "Is that what you mean?"

"Is that what you want?" she countered. "Separate rooms?"

"Oh, Susan, *Susan,*" he whispered with a half-exasperated sigh. "I think you know very well what *I* want and it simply cannot be accomplished if we sleep in different rooms."

His wry tone brought a tremulous smile to her lips.

"Well, then, I do have a very comfortable bed, if you'd like to share it."

"I hope you don't expect me to refuse that offer," he

muttered roughly, his eyes half closed and aglow with passion as he pulled her closer. "Maybe I should say I can wait until Saturday, but I just can't. I've wanted you too long."

"Then love me, Adam," she invited, slipping her hands beneath his sweater, moving her fingers caressingly across his muscular chest. "I want you to love me now, tonight."

With a muffled exclamation, he crushed her to him, taking her mouth with devastating force, rubbing the tip of his tongue over her lips until they parted wide and her body was yielding to the exploration of his urgent hands.

Breathing quickly, he pulled back, his smile a promise as he easily undid the tie belt of her robe. And though Susan suddenly trembled, he relentlessly pushed aside the lapels with slow deliberation, almost as if he realized her weakening body was burning with anticipation.

"Oh, Susan, you are exquisite!" he whispered hoarsely, his lean brown hand cupping the ivory fullness of her breast, which swelled to his touch. His fingers caressed the taut satiny skin, tracing small circles around the rose-tipped peak until she was aching with desire for him.

"Adam, oh, I love you so much," she breathed, sliding her arms around his neck, pressing her slender body close against him. And when his hands moved searchingly down her back to cover her hips, she sought his mouth eagerly with her own.

His lips took hers with bruising force as he laid a possessive hand across her abdomen, stroking the sensitive skin with gentle yet insistent fingers.

"Where is your room?" he asked roughly, lowering her feet to the floor and standing, impelling her to stand also. Drawing her to him, he pressed her hips against his thighs, allowing her to feel his surging passionate response. And when she took a swift, sharp breath of acknowledgment, he swept her up in his arms. "Your room?"

"Upstairs," she murmured, burrowing her face against his neck as he strode out into the hall toward the steps. She could only cling weakly to him, her slight body trembling in his arms, as he stopped by the door to her room.

"Look at me," he commanded gently, smiling down into her suddenly shy eyes as she met his dark gaze. "You're afraid of me, aren't you? Please don't be."

She smiled tremulously, her breath catching as he bent his head to kiss her lingeringly, persuasively, until all her remaining fears were lost in the passion he aroused. And as he carried her into her room she whispered against his lips, "I guess we have turned out like Jonathan and Felicity after all, haven't we?"

"Only up to a point," he whispered back softly. "The difference is I *won't* be a reluctant bridegroom come Saturday and you'll be a very well loved bride," he qualified with a teasing smile. And when an enchanting pink blush tinted her cheeks, his lips sought hers again as he kicked the bedroom door shut with his foot.

Silhouette Romance

ROMANCE THE WAY
IT USED TO BE...
AND COULD BE AGAIN

Contemporary romances for today's women.

Each month, six very special love stories will be yours

from SILHOUETTE.

Look for them wherever books are sold

or order now from the coupon below.

$1.50 each

<table>
<tr><td>___ # 1 PAYMENT IN FULL Hampson</td><td>___ #25 SHADOW OF LOVE Stanford</td></tr>
<tr><td>___ # 2 SHADOW AND SUN Carroll</td><td>___ #26 INNOCENT FIRE Hastings</td></tr>
<tr><td>___ # 3 AFFAIRS OF THE HEART Powers</td><td>___ #27 THE DAWN STEALS SOFTLY Hampson</td></tr>
<tr><td>___ # 4 STORMY MASQUERADE Hampson</td><td>___ #28 MAN OF THE OUTBACK Hampson</td></tr>
<tr><td>___ # 5 PATH OF DESIRE Goforth</td><td>___ #29 RAIN LADY Wildman</td></tr>
<tr><td>___ # 6 GOLDEN TIDE Stanford</td><td>___ #30 RETURN ENGAGEMENT Dixon</td></tr>
<tr><td>___ # 7 MIDSUMMER BRIDE Lewis</td><td>___ #31 TEMPORARY BRIDE Halldorson</td></tr>
<tr><td>___ # 8 CAPTIVE HEART Beckman</td><td>___ #32 GOLDEN LASSO Michaels</td></tr>
<tr><td>___ # 9 WHERE MOUNTAINS WAIT Wilson</td><td>___ #33 A DIFFERENT DREAM Vitek</td></tr>
<tr><td>___ #10 BRIDGE OF LOVE Caine</td><td>___ #34 THE SPANISH HOUSE John</td></tr>
<tr><td>___ #11 AWAKEN THE HEART Vernon</td><td>___ #35 STORM'S END Stanford</td></tr>
<tr><td>___ #12 UNREASONABLE SUMMER Browning</td><td>___ #36 BRIDAL TRAP McKay</td></tr>
<tr><td>___ #13 PLAYING FOR KEEPS Hastings</td><td>___ #37 THE BEACHCOMBER Beckman</td></tr>
<tr><td>___ #14 RED, RED ROSE Oliver</td><td>___ #38 TUMBLED WALL Browning</td></tr>
<tr><td>___ #15 SEA GYPSY Michaels</td><td>___ #39 PARADISE ISLAND Sinclair</td></tr>
<tr><td>___ #16 SECOND TOMORROW Hampson</td><td>___ #40 WHERE EAGLES NEST Hampson</td></tr>
<tr><td>___ #17 TORMENTING FLAME John</td><td>___ #41 THE SANDS OF TIME Owen</td></tr>
<tr><td>___ #18 THE LION'S SHADOW Hunter</td><td>___ #42 DESIGN FOR LOVE Powers</td></tr>
<tr><td>___ #19 THE HEART NEVER FORGETS Thornton</td><td>___ #43 SURRENDER IN PARADISE Robb</td></tr>
<tr><td>___ #20 ISLAND DESTINY Fulford</td><td>___ #44 DESERT FIRE Hastings</td></tr>
<tr><td>___ #21 SPRING FIRES Richards</td><td>___ #45 TOO SWIFT THE MORNING Carroll</td></tr>
<tr><td>___ #22 MEXICAN NIGHTS Stephens</td><td>___ #46 NO TRESPASSING Stanford</td></tr>
<tr><td>___ #23 BEWITCHING GRACE Edwards</td><td>___ #47 SHOWERS OF SUNLIGHT Vitek</td></tr>
<tr><td>___ #24 SUMMER STORM Healy</td><td>___ #48 A RACE FOR LOVE Wildman</td></tr>
</table>

Silhouette Romance

__ #49 DANCER IN THE SHADOWS Wisdom	__ #60 GREEN PARADISE Hill
__ #50 DUSKY ROSE Scott	__ #61 WHISPER MY NAME Michaels
__ #51 BRIDE OF THE SUN Hunter	__ #62 STAND-IN BRIDE Halston
__ #52 MAN WITHOUT A HEART Hampson	__ #63 SNOWFLAKES IN THE SUN Brent
__ #53 CHANCE TOMORROW Browning	__ #64 SHADOW OF APOLLO Hampson
__ #54 LOUISIANA LADY Beckman	__ #65 A TOUCH OF MAGIC Hunter
__ #55 WINTER'S HEART Ladame	__ #66 PROMISES FROM THE PAST Vitek
__ #56 RISING STAR Trent	__ #67 ISLAND CONQUEST Hastings
__ #57 TO TRUST TOMORROW John	__ #68 THE MARRIAGE BARGAIN Scott
__ #58 LONG WINTER'S NIGHT Stanford	__ #69 WEST OF THE MOON St. George
__ #59 KISSED BY MOONLIGHT Vernon	

- -

SILHOUETTE BOOKS. Department SB/1
1230 Avenue of the Americas
New York, NY 10020

Please send me the books I have checked above. I am enclosing
$_____ (please add 50¢ to cover postage and handling for each
order. NYS and NYC residents please add appropriate sales tax).
Send check or money order—no cash or C.O.D.s please. Allow six
weeks for delivery.

NAME_____

ADDRESS_____

CITY_____STATE/ZIP_____

Silhouette Romance

15-Day Free Trial Offer
6 Silhouette Romances

6 Silhouette Romances, free for 15 days! We'll send you 6 new Silhouette Romances to keep for 15 days, absolutely free! If you decide not to keep them, send them back to us. We'll pay the return postage. You pay nothing.

Free Home Delivery. But if you enjoy them as much as we think you will, keep them by paying us the retail price of just $1.50 each. We'll pay all shipping and handling charges. You'll then automatically become a member of the Silhouette Book Club, and will receive 6 more new Silhouette Romances every month and a bill for $9.00. That's the same price you'd pay in the store, but you get the convenience of home delivery.

Read every book we publish. The Silhouette Book Club is the way to make sure you'll be able to receive every new romance we publish.

This offer expires July 31, 1981

Silhouette Book Club, Dept. SBB17B
120 Brighton Road, Clifton, NJ 07012

Please send me 6 Silhouette Romances to keep for 15 days, absolutely free. I understand I am not obligated to join the Silhouette Book Club unless I decide to keep them.

NAME_____

ADDRESS_____

CITY_____ STATE_____ ZIP_____

READERS' COMMENTS ON SILHOUETTE ROMANCES:

"You give us joy and surprises throughout the books . . . they're the best books I've read."
—J.S.*, Crosby, MN

"Needless to say I am addicted to your books. . . . I love the characters, the settings, the emotions."
—V.D., Plane, TX

"Every one was written with the utmost care. The story of each captures one's interest early in the plot and holds it through until the end."
—P.B., Summersville, WV

"I get so carried away with the books I forget the time."
—L.W., Beltsville, MD

"Silhouette has a great talent for picking winners."
—K.W., Detroit, MI

* names available on request.